# WHERE DO YOU STAY?

# where
# do
# you
# stay?

## ANDREA CHENG

BOYDS MILLS PRESS
*Honesdale, Pennsylvania*

ISBN: 978-1-59078-707-6

Library of Congress Control Number: 2010938271

Boyds Mills Press, Inc.
815 Church Street
Honesdale, Pennsylvania 18431

10 9 8 7 6 5 4 3 2 1

*To the memory of my father*

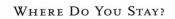

WHERE DO YOU STAY?

# 1

Mr. Willie pulls every last weed in the driveway cracks, then sweeps the concrete clean. Aunt Geneva comes out to pay him, but Mr. Willie doesn't want any money. "A sandwich would be nice," he says.

"Are you sure?" She holds out the dollar bills, but Mr. Willie shakes his head.

Aunt Geneva makes two peanut butter and jam sandwiches, slices up an apple, and puts it all into a lunch bag. "Jerome, you take these out to Mr. Willie," she says.

He's sitting on the ground under the ginkgo tree. "Aunt Geneva said to give this to you." I hand him the bag. He lays out his lunch all in order, then eats steady, not in a hurry but not stopping either. When he finishes both sandwiches and the apple, he uses the bag to wipe his mouth.

"Where do you stay at, Mr. Willie?" I ask.

He shows me with his chin. "Up the hill. What about you?"

He's never seen me before because I haven't been here long. "My name's Jerome and I just finished the fifth grade. Now I'm staying with my Aunt Geneva and

Uncle James," I tell him. His eyes are closed. "Since my mother passed."

Mr. Willie nods.

"I could stay with Aunt Melinda, but she lives in New York."

I'm not sure if Mr. Willie heard me or not.

"And I have two more aunts in Atlanta."

"You say New York?"

"Yes. New York City. Aunt Melinda lives there. But Mama said it would be best not to go far."

Mr. Willie lies down to take a nap.

# 2

"That old man's crazy," my cousin Damon says. "Walking up and down the street, pulling weeds."

"Why's that crazy?"

"You want to be doing that when you're old?" He turns to his little brother, Monte. "Jerome's going to be a bum."

"I never said that."

Damon is dribbling a basketball between his legs and behind his back. He's tall for fifteen, with arms so long they're everywhere at once. He sends the ball my way. It hits my leg, bounces into the street, and starts rolling down the hill. Damon stops it with his foot. "Come on," he says to his brother, heading toward the basketball rim nailed to a telephone pole.

Damon makes the first shot. Monte gets the rebound, tries for a lay-up, and misses. Damon has the ball again.

I head across the street.

Mr. Willie is behind the carriage house digging with a piece of rusty metal. I go close so I can see in the hole. There's something white in there. "What is it?" I ask.

"We're about to find out," he says, handing me a tool just like his.

"Where'd you get this big old nail?" I ask.

Mr. Willie smiles and I see that lots of his teeth are gone. "Called a railroad spike," he says.

I start digging as fast as I can. I move the clods of clay to the side with my hands so I can see what I'm doing. The sweat is dripping down my forehead, stinging my eyes. Mama said *Dig the garden deep so the carrots grow sweet.* We added sand to break up the clay, mixed in compost too. Rotten banana peels and eggshells and onion skins.

"Slow down, Jerome," Mr. Willie says. "Don't hit too close or you might chip it."

I didn't know he even remembered my name. "Chip what?" I ask.

"Can't know for sure quite yet. But I do have an idea."

I'm careful after that, trying to match Mr. Willie's steady rhythm. We have to make the hole wider before we can get down deep.

Damon and Monte are standing there. "You digging to China, Jerome?" Damon asks.

"Does this look like China?" I ask.

"Never been there," Monte says.

Damon kicks at the dirt. "Come on," he says to his brother.

"Wait," Monte says, looking into the hole.

"Wait for what?" Damon bounces the ball on the ground right next to the hole, making dirt fall back in.

"Stop it," I say.

"There's something white in there," Monte says.

"Nothing but rocks." Damon grabs Monte's arm and pulls him away. He's whispering something about Mr. Willie being crazy, or me being crazy, or both.

"Your brothers?" Mr. Willie asks after they're finally gone.

"Cousins."

"Miss Geneva's boys?"

"Yup. I'm staying there now."

"You said."

He doesn't ask why or how long or anything. Our hole's getting wider but it's hard to keep the dirt from falling back and water's starting to come up from below like it does.

"Could use a shovel," Mr. Willie says.

"I'll get us one."

# 3

Damon and Monte are sitting on the couch watching television. "Do you have a shovel?" I ask.

Damon turns the volume up.

Aunt Geneva is cutting potatoes. "What do you need a shovel for?" she asks.

"I'm helping Mr. Willie," I say.

"Damon, turn off that television," Aunt Geneva says.

He turns the volume down, but he's still watching.

"You heard me," she says.

He turns it off and glares at me.

"Now one of you go and get the shovel out of the basement," Aunt Geneva says. "You know where it hangs behind the door."

Damon looks at his brother. Monte stares back.

"If one of you doesn't get the shovel, neither of you are watching that TV for a long while," Aunt Geneva says.

Monte kicks at the floor, then goes down the basement steps and comes up with a long-handled shovel.

"What are you helping Mr. Willie with?" Aunt Geneva asks.

"Jerome's digging to China," Monte says.

"Better than wasting your mind on that television," Aunt Geneva says. She looks at me. "Your mother raised you right."

I wish she wouldn't say that because it makes Damon mad. He's rolling his eyes. I hurry up the hill with the shovel dragging.

Mr. Willie uses the shovel to pile the dirt into a neat mound. I keep chipping with the railroad spike. We're starting to see more of the white stone. It's rounded on top, like a head, like a dead man's skull except it looks to me like there's curls on the head, and dead people don't have hair. Sometimes living people don't either, like Mama before she passed. Aunt Melinda gave her a wig to wear but I said *I don't like that wig, it doesn't look like you with that wig on,* and Mama said *A bald head scares people, Jerome,* and I said *Not me, the wig scares me.*

"Time to take a break," Mr. Willie says. He leans the shovel against the wall, goes into the carriage house, and comes out with a thermos, two cups, and a bag of carrots. I drink the cold water and bite a carrot, but it's not sweet like the ones Mama used to grow.

"Do you stay right here?" I point to the carriage house.

Mr. Willie nods.

"I'm staying with Aunt Geneva and Uncle James," I say. I pour myself another cup of water.

"You said." Mr. Willie looks at me like I can say more if I want or not if I don't.

"We didn't think she'd go this quick."

"Hard to predict," Mr. Willie says.

"What's hard to predict?"

"When people are born and when they die and all that's in between." He takes a long drink and pours us both some more. "Your Aunt Geneva makes a good sandwich," he says.

"Her chili is good too. I'll bring you some next time."

"That would be nice."

"Can you cook in there?" I point to the carriage house.

Mr. Willie nods.

"Is there a kitchen?"

"Of sorts."

"Do people know you stay here?"

"Nobody's business," he says.

I know that's right. When Mama passed, everyone was in my business. They said they could find my daddy and I could stay with him, but he'd been gone so long, who even knew where he was. Mama didn't, that's for sure. We were a temporary stop, she said, a place for him to stay. *Maybe he'll be back*, I said. Mama held me close. *Or maybe not. No matter, Jerome. We're fine here the two of us, we know that.*

I could go to my aunt's in New York and see the Empire State Building and all that. Aunt Geneva said *No, that boy isn't going anywhere far away like that. He's staying with me like his mother wanted. He's our boy now.* I felt my breakfast come up in my throat. I'm not anybody's boy. I'm Jerome Mason, I'm going in the sixth grade, and I play piano.

The main thing was I didn't want Mama in that coffin with that wig that made her look like a witch. The funeral-home man said *Don't you want your mama to look pretty?* I said *She looks ugly with that ugly wig.* Finally Aunt Geneva said *Listen to the boy, it's his business,* and the funeral-home man took it off.

Mr. Willie gives me a bandana like his to keep the sweat from stinging my eyes and we go back to our digging, but my eyes are burning like fire. Mama said *Sure, Jerome, it's good to think, to consider, but too much thinking is called mulling. You know that word, Jerome?* Mulling is like tires spinning on ice, turning around real fast but getting nowhere. I know Mama's right, but for some reason the digging makes a lump grow in my throat so big I can hardly swallow.

Some of the neighborhood kids come by to see what we're doing. "You're Damon and Monte's cousin, aren't you," a girl named Ashley asks.

I nod.

"How old are you?"

"Eleven."

"Older than Monte."

"Yup."

"You staying here now?"

"I guess."

4

It's whiter than any stone I've ever seen.

"Marble," Mr. Willie says. "There's white marble, black marble, and pink marble. This here's white, same as the steps."

"What steps?"

We sit back for a minute and Mr. Willie closes his eyes. "On hot days in the big house, I'd lie on one marble step until my skin heated up and then move up to the next until I got to the top, and then I'd start all over again. My mother said, 'Wilson, get up off there and do something,' but Miss Myrtle said, 'Leave him, he's listening.'"

"I didn't know your real name was Wilson."

"Still is."

"Do you want me to call you Mr. Wilson, then?"

"No matter." Mr. Willie adjusts his bandana. "Long as I know it's me you're talking to."

"I like to be called Jerome. Not Jerry."

"Jerome it is, then."

"Who's Miss Myrtle?" I ask.

"She was the lady of the house." Mr. Willie looks up at the big mansion with the windows all busted out and boarded up. "My mother worked there."

"In that house?"

Mr. Willie nods. "We came every morning."

"Did you ever sleep in there?"

Mr. Willie considers. "It might have happened a couple of times. Generally we went home at night to sleep in our own beds."

"Just you and your mother?"

Mr. Willie nods. "The two of us."

"Like me and Mama," I say. Mama never planned on having a big family anyway. No need for a crowd, she said. We sat on the porch and watched David across the street with his three brothers and three sisters and two cats and one dog. *That's more than I could handle,* Mama said.

"This here was the carriage house," Mr. Willie says.

"Were there carriages inside?"

"Before my time." Mr. Willie is digging and talking at once. "Miss Myrtle kept her car in here." He laughs. "But she couldn't drive it."

"What'd she have a car for, then?"

"Mr. James, the chauffeur, he drove Sharon here and there and everywhere."

"Sharon?"

"Miss Myrtle's daughter. A couple of months younger than me. We used to play together. Except when Miss Myrtle made her go in and practice the piano. That's when I sat on the marble steps."

"I play the piano," I say.

Mr. Willie stops digging. "For some reason, that doesn't surprise me."

"My mother started teaching me when I was five. She said I could pick out tunes soon as I was old enough to talk." Daddy was there then, sitting on the sofa next to Mama with the light coming in like a rainbow through the front window. *That boy has talent,* Mama told him. *Listen.*

"I was older than that, maybe nine or ten by the time I started. Sharon's teacher gave me a few minutes at the end of each lesson." Mr. Willie smiles wide and I see the gaps where his teeth were. "We were quite a team back then, me and Sharon. We were going to play tunes for four hands all over the country." Mr. Willie sweeps his hand.

"Mama and I played duets too." We were planning to have concerts someday in a real concert hall with a grand piano. I close my eyes. Mama had cataracts so bad at the end she could only see light and dark. *Long as I don't go deaf,* she used to tell me, *I'll be okay. I need music and I need talking too.* I swear, she could hear us even in that coffin, arguing about her wig.

"Does Miss Geneva have a piano?" Mr. Willie asks.

"Monte says they're going to get one." Suddenly I have this urge to play the Chopin prelude Mama liked so much. "Do you think Sharon's piano might still be inside the big house?"

Mr. Willie shakes his head. "Long gone by now."

"Gone where?"

"Stolen. Sold. The house is just a shell of itself by now." He looks over at the mansion with boards cockeyed where the windows were. "It's been empty a good while, Jerome, since long before you were born." He thinks for a minute. "Let's see, Sharon must have left about 1930."

"My daddy left too," I say. "A few years back."

"People are most unpredictable," Mr. Willie says.

Mama told Aunt Melinda that Daddy sent her a post-card from Nashville, and I said *Let's go down there and look in the telephone book for William Mason,* and Mama said *No, Jerome, no need to look for someone who doesn't want to be found.*

Mr. Willie stares at the mansion. "The church took it over for their school. That lasted some number of years, and then it closed down for good." Mr. Willie wipes his forehead. "You didn't know you were going to get a history lesson today, did you?"

"My mother said there's history in everything, in our bones even."

"I know that's right." Mr. Willie stops to look at a rock. "You ever heard of white flight, Jerome?"

"My mother told me about that too."

"That's what happened around here." Mr. Willie squints up at the old house. "Nobody wants to buy a big old mansion like this anymore." He laughs. "It would cost a pretty penny to fix it up and then to heat it in the wintertime. And people with that kind of money are staying far away from here."

I stand up and look down the street. The houses are big with paint flaking off and rusty mailboxes nailed to the front doors. The yards are full of poison ivy plants as healthy as I've ever seen. On my old street the houses were small but neat. Most everyone had window boxes filled with flowers on their porches. Mama liked petunias best. *What color, Jerome? Purple and white? You have a good eye, you know that?* When the flowers got too heavy, Mama snipped them with scissors. I collected the blossoms and put them in a bowl of water.

"I'm telling you," Mr. Willie says, "in its day, that house was magnificent."

"Maybe we can fix it up," I say.

Mr. Willie shakes his head. "That will take more than a broom and a dustpan."

If we fixed up the mansion, there'd be room for as many pianos as we wanted. We could invite Aunt Geneva and Uncle James and the boys and David with his brothers and three sisters to listen to our duets. *We can hear you playing the piano from our house,* David said. *I wish I could stay with you and your mother because it's peaceful at your house, Jerome, and there's always music coming through the windows.*

Mr. Willie is digging deep, trying to unearth whatever it is.

# 5

My fingers are getting sore from scraping the dirt, but we're making progress now. We got the hair pretty much uncovered.

"What kind of music did you play?" I ask.

"Started with the scales, arpeggios, you know, those exercise books." Mr. Willie's eyes cloud over like Mama's used to. "Then I went on to learn the classics. Miss Myrtle was so proud of me she told my mother I should get music lessons, and Mama said, 'He's getting them right here.' Miss Myrtle said, 'No, I mean in a real music conservatory,' and Mama said, 'Maybe someday.'"

"Did you?"

Mr. Willie nods. "Sure did." He wipes his forehead with a handkerchief. Then he gets the thermos and pours the last bit of water into our cups. We drink it fast.

"So why'd you quit?"

"Quit what?"

"Playing the piano."

"Quit? No, I never quit. I'd sit down right now and play if we had a piano. I didn't quit anything. Just life got in the way, Jerome, like this dirt here's in the way, making it hard to get this marble sculpture out of the ground."

People dying gets in the way too. If Mama was here we could play our duets and with the money we earned we could buy a baby grand the way we planned. I said *Then maybe Daddy will come back*, and Mama said *No, Jerome, don't think like that, he's not interested*. In music? I asked. *In us*, she said.

Our shirts are drenched and clinging to our skin, and we're working fast. It's a white marble head with wavy hair and two eyes. I stop, scared for a second that there's some dead man I'm digging up. Mr. Willie laughs. "You know what a sculpture is, Jerome? This here is called a bust."

"Whose head is it?"

"One of the three B's."

"You mean Bach, Beethoven, and Brahms?"

Mr. Willie sits back on his heels. "You know your music, don't you?"

Finally he gets his long fingers underneath and lifts that bust up out of the ground, gentle like a baby. He rubs the chin to get the mud off.

"Well, I'll be ... I almost forgot all about you, Mr. Beethoven." He carries the head over to the hose poking out from between bushes and turns the nozzle, and we let the cold water run all over the hair, the eyes, the chipped nose, the thin lips. The marble shines in the afternoon sun. "See these darker lines in the marble? They're called veins."

"Just like our veins," I say, looking at the back of Mr. Willie's knobby hands. "Except without the blood."

Mama had those popping out veins too, only hers were bruised from nurses sticking needles in. Slippery veins, one nurse said, like it was Mama's fault.

"Ludwig van Beethoven," Willie whispers.

"That's really what he looked like?" I ask. The hair is what I like best, big waves that look soft though it's solid marble.

Mr. Willie shuts his eyes. "Miss Myrtle had these sitting on the piano. Said they'd inspire us while we played." Mr. Willie moves his long fingers over the cheeks, the jaw, the strong neck. "Mr. Beethoven was deaf, but the music was inside," he says.

"I like the Ninth Symphony," I say.

Mr. Willie hums the first few measures. "And how he could write that kind of music and never hear it, now that's a wonder."

The sun's just going down and that sculpture is shining like it is brand-new. "How'd Mr. Beethoven get buried in all this dirt?" I ask.

"That I don't know."

Aunt Geneva's calling.

Mr. Willie is trying to get the dirt out from in between the curls with his fingernails. "You better get on home, Jerome. I got a feeling Miss Geneva's not one to wait."

"Do you think Bach and Brahms are buried here too?" I'm thinking when I get my own piano someday, I'll set those busts on top.

"Could be. Or not."

"How did you know to dig right here?" I ask.

"I was just digging to plant some seeds," Mr. Willie says. "And I know marble when I see it."

"But what—"

Aunt Geneva calls again.

Mr. Willie's eyes meet mine. "Go on home now, Jerome."

I stand up. Mr. Willie said home, but Aunt Geneva's house is not my home. My home is over on the other side of town in the small house with purple and white petunias and an upright soon as you walk in, then the dining room and the kitchen opening out to the back where we dug our garden. Mama said *We'll plant the tomatoes along the fence, Jerome. No need for stakes if we've got a fence to tie them to. We'll put the cucumbers in front.* Aunt Geneva has a clump of wilting black-eyed Susans near the gate. *Your mother got the green thumb,* she says. *She got the piano hands and the brains. She got it all, Jerome.*

My mother got cancer too.

"Better hurry up," Mr. Willie says, looking straight at me.

I run down the hill.

# 6

There are two beds for the three of us. After the funeral I slept in Damon's bed, but he said it wasn't fair, him being older, so I moved over to Monte's. He said I took up too much room. I *am* big compared to their skinny bald-headed selves.

I make a bed for myself in the corner on some blankets. Aunt Geneva comes in and starts hollering. "Who taught you boys that kind of meanness, I'd like to know? I know it wasn't me."

Damon's hiding under the blankets.

"I never said he couldn't sleep with me," Monte says.

Aunt Geneva goes over and whips those covers off Damon's head. Then she tells both her boys to get up off the beds and sleep on the floor, and she tells me I can have my pick of beds or I can sleep across both of them if I'd like. She says she'll get a third bed, soon as Uncle James brings his next paycheck. "Things happened faster than I anticipated," she says.

But I don't want to sleep in beds that smell like Damon and Monte, so when Aunt Geneva goes downstairs, I go back to my corner. They are afraid their mother will come back, so they take some blankets and curl up in two other corners and the beds are left empty.

It occurs to me that Mr. Willie might like to sleep in one, him being so old and everything, but he has a place all to himself in the carriage house. And now he's got Mr. Beethoven to keep him company.

I move my fingers under the sheet, right hand going up, left hand going down and I start humming that song, that last one Mama taught me, a duet for four hands by Grieg, and before you know it, I'm sniffling and I can't stop.

Aunt Geneva comes up again. "You tell me, Jerome, what'd they do this time? You can tell me the truth." She's holding me in her arms that are much fatter than Mama's skinny stick arms. "Your mama raised you better than I can raise these two that I have."

"They didn't do anything," I say finally.

"You wouldn't be crying for nothing." Then she says, "Jerome, you come over here and sleep on this bed like I told you." She smoothes the sheet out and I lie down real stiff in the middle of Monte's bed. She lets the sheet fall gently on my sweaty skin.

I feel Aunt Geneva's hand rubbing my back. "Now think about your mama in heaven. She's in a better place now, Jerome, a better place for sure." I don't want Aunt Geneva talking about heaven when Mama never did. I'm sniffling and she's sniffling and Damon and Monte too. Her hand is rubbing my shoulders, my neck, smoothing out the pajama shirt. "Your mama made plans for you, you know that."

Me and Mama were sitting on the couch, watching the

morning sun. She said *Jerome, you won't ever be alone,* and I said *Long as I have a piano, I'm okay,* and she said *No, Little Man, you aren't grown up yet. You're going to stay with Aunt Geneva and Uncle James and their boys.* And I said *For how long?* Mama said *We can't plan that far ahead.*

Aunt Geneva is breathing hard, trying not to cry. "Your mama wouldn't want us sitting here and bawling our eyes out. You know what she'd say, don't you?"

Mama said lots of things. *Enough,* she'd say, *now that's enough, Jerome. Pity only goes so far.* Or *Get busy, Jerome. Busy hands heal a heart.* Mama said all that.

Aunt Geneva sighs. "When I was a little girl and your mother was just a year older, we found a baby rabbit. We tried to feed it all kinds of things, but it wouldn't eat. Just too little, I think. Or maybe it was sick. I held it in my hands and felt its tiny heart fluttering. And then it stopped. We buried that rabbit in the backyard under a rock. I cried for days. Just couldn't stop thinking about that last breath. Finally your mother had enough of my sniffling, and she said, 'Geneva, you see all these trees and flowers growing out of this dirt? This dirt comes from all the living things that died over the years. So if they didn't die, there'd be nothing alive.' 'Even me?' I asked. 'Even you,' she said. And I stopped crying."

Aunt Geneva tells Monte and Damon to say sorry to me, so they mumble something. Then she goes downstairs to make soup for when Uncle James gets home from working a double shift.

Mama's under all that dirt and turning into dirt. The worms are helping. Earthworms are the best thing a garden can have, Mama said. I know they put her in a coffin, but that coffin's wood, and wood will turn into dirt eventually. Just give it time. Good thing they finally took that plastic wig off Mama's head before they shut the coffin. Ms. Simmons said *This wig looks better even than her real hair. And it is real hair, imported from China.* But Mama said the wig was itchy and tight so soon as it was just me and her, she yanked that wig off her bald head and we sat on the sofa together. She said *Jerome, play me that Grieg we've been working on,* and I said *It's for four hands,* and she said *I know but I'm tired, so you just play the one part and then the other and we'll put the parts together in our heads.*

When Mama was asleep, I tiptoed over and picked that wig up off the floor. The hair might have been real, but it was glued onto something stiff and itchy and plastic. And plastic doesn't turn into dirt very fast, I know that.

In the morning, Mama wasn't breathing. All the neighbors were there. Ms. Simmons put that wig on Mama's head and I said *No, she doesn't like it, take it off.* Ms. Simmons said *Shhh, Jerome, shhhhh,* but I wouldn't give up because I was the only one who really knew what Mama wanted.

I'm playing the piano on the mattress and humming a tune at the same time. Damon whispers something to Monte, asking if I'm staying for the whole summer, and Monte says I'm staying forever. Damon turns to me. "Are you?" he whispers.

I say, "I sure hope not because you all don't even have a piano."

Damon covers his head with the sheet.

Maybe I'll move in with Mr. Willie because nobody would bother me there even if I was humming and moving my fingers around. He wouldn't have a problem with that. We'll go into that mansion and find the piano that must be there. One at a time we'll fix up those rooms with fresh plaster walls and new pipes until it's good as new. And when it's done, we'll have a concert and invite everyone we know.

7

Mr. Willie's frying fish that smells so good. His fishing pole is leaning against the stone wall, and he's holding the skillet over a small fire.

"What kind of fish is that?" I ask.

"Catfish," he says. "A nice big one."

Damon and Monte come with me because they can smell that fish all the way down the hill. "Where'd you catch it?" Monte asks.

"Mill Creek."

Monte looks at his brother. "That water's nasty," Damon says. "Full of chemicals and stuff."

"I've been eating fish out of the Mill Creek for sixty years," Mr. Willie says. He takes the skillet off the fire, kicks some dirt onto the burning log, and turns the fish out onto a plate. Then he hands us each a fork.

"Maybe we shouldn't eat this Mill Creek fish," Monte says.

Mr. Willie says, "Suit yourself, but if you eat it, watch for the bones."

Monte takes a nibble, and Damon and me too. That is the best fish I ever tasted. Mr. Willie says when he used to work on the loading dock, he caught bigger fish, Ohio River bass, catfish, you name it.

When we're done, Mr. Willie rinses the bones off the plate in the hose. Monte says, "You live in this old carriage house?"

Mr. Willie doesn't answer.

"Who pays for that water coming out of the hose?" Damon asks.

"That's Ms. Jackson's hose and Ms. Jackson's water," Mr. Willie says. He stands up straight. "I cut her grass, she gives me water."

"You have a bathroom in there?" Monte asks.

"You boys have a lot of questions today," Mr. Willie says.

"Is there one?" Monte asks.

"There's a toilet and a shower in Ms. Jackson's basement, if you have to know."

"They're going to tear this whole place down," Damon says.

Mr. Willie stiffens. "Who told you that?"

"Everybody knows. There's the sign." He points over to the mansion, and sure enough, there's a small black-and-white For Sale sign stuck into the ground right in front.

"Selling it doesn't mean tearing it down," I say.

Damon laughs. "So, what do you think they'll do?"

"Fix it up," I say.

"Nothing left to fix," Damon says. He kicks at a rock. "Mama says whoever buys it will level it for sure."

"What's 'level it' mean?" Monte asks.

Damon sweeps his arm to show us. "They'll bring in a bulldozer, knock all this down, and haul it away."

"You mean the big house too?" Monte asks.

Damon shrugs. "Probably."

"I didn't hear Aunt Geneva say that," I say.

He crosses his arms on his chest. "If you didn't spend all your time up here digging in this dirt, maybe you'd hear something."

I look at over at Mr. Willie and his chin is quivering. "If the church is selling Miss Myrtle's house," he says softly, "somebody ought to at least let Sharon know."

"Who's Sharon?" Monte asks.

"She used to live here," I say. "A long time ago."

Damon kicks at the wall and a stone falls off the side. "Everyone knows this place is an eyesore," he says. He drags that word out. Eyesore, makes your eyes sore. Nothing ever makes my eyes sore, but Damon makes my head ache. "And it's haunted too," he says.

"No such thing," I say. *Don't believe that kind of talk, Jerome,* Mama said. *That's just people trying to scare you.*

Damon laughs. "I dare you to come up here on Halloween," he says, narrowing his eyes.

Mr. Willie stands up straight so he's even taller than Damon. "Whoever says that house is an eyesore has never been inside. The floor is inlaid with different colored pieces of wood, some teak, some cherry. You know what a mosaic is? That's what's on that floor. And the windows are stained glass with leaded panes." Mr. Willie has his eyes shut, remembering.

"There's not a single window pane in that whole building," Damon says.

"And the steps of white marble, so cool on my skin." Mr. Willie drops his head, goes over to the hose, and splashes water onto his face. He comes back to where the fishing pole is leaning against the carriage house. "It does need some work," he says, picking up the stone that Damon knocked loose and setting it back where it belongs.

"Come on," Damon says to his brother. I know he's thinking *Let's leave those two alone, they're so crazy.* Some of the other neighborhood kids are hanging around by the basketball net.

Monte looks like he wants to stay.

"Come on," Damon says again. He grabs his brother by the shirt and drags him down the hill.

8

Mr. Willie puts some water into a bucket, adds a little cement, and mixes it with a small trowel.

"We better hurry and fix this place up," he says.

"What if they really do tear it down?" I ask.

"That's why we better get fixing," Mr. Willie says. "So they can see the beauty in the stone work." He drops a glob of cement onto the top of the wall, sets a stone in it, and smoothes off the extra.

I watch for a minute, then pick up a stone and set it into the next glob of cement. We work like that until we finish the row.

"When the wall is done, we'll work on the vegetable garden," Mr. Willie says.

"My mother said I have a green thumb," I say. "We had a nice garden alongside our fence with tomatoes and cucumbers and carrots."

"A green thumb goes with the music," Mr. Willie says.

"It does?"

"Piano fingers and a green thumb." Mr. Willie scrapes the last bit of cement out of the bucket. "Go hand in hand."

Suddenly there's a question I have to ask. "Mr. Willie?"

"What is it?"

"Where are you going to stay if they really do tear this place down?"

Mr. Willie walks over to the hose and rinses out the bucket. "I'll cross that bridge when I come to it."

"But what if you're inside when they come with the bulldozer?"

Mr. Willie sets the bucket upside down to dry. "A bulldozer makes plenty of noise. And my ears are plenty good."

"But where would you stay after that?" My eyes are burning again and I don't even really know why. Too much mulling, thinking about Mama and our garden and how Mr. Willie could have stayed with us on our fold-out cot in the living room with the piano right close by.

"I'll figure something out," Mr. Willie says.

I wanted to keep on living in my old house. I could have gotten up and fixed myself oatmeal for breakfast, then walked to school with David. I'd need some kind of job to buy my clothes, but I could grow carrots and beans and cucumbers to eat. David's mother wouldn't care if I came for dinner now and then. And if I got good enough, I could play the piano for celebrations like weddings to earn a little money. But Mama said *No, Jerome, you're not grown yet.* Aunt Geneva said I'd be going to a new school anyway for the sixth grade because my old school stopped at fifth.

*You're our boy now, Jerome,* she said, without even asking my permission.

Mr. Willie rinses the bucket under the hose. Then we stretch a piece of string to mark the edges of the vegetable garden. Mr. Willie turns over the dirt with the shovel and I break up the clods with the railroad spike.

"We could fix up the mansion," I say suddenly. Mr. Willie puts his weight on the shovel and turns over the soil, but I can tell he's listening. "We could both stay there."

Mr. Willie's eyes meet mine. "It's not ours to fix," he says.

"It's not doing anybody much good just sitting empty," I say.

Mr. Willie places the shovel again. "You're staying with your Aunt Geneva," he says.

A lump is growing in my throat. "Nobody asked me what I wanted."

"Your Aunt Geneva is one of the kindest people I know," Mr. Willie says. "She's helped me out on more than one occasion."

I hit the clods of dirt, one after the other with the railroad spike. I can fix that mansion up by myself, one room at a time, that's what I'll do. I'll live in there where nobody can tell me what to do. I'll find that piano and play all night if I feel like it and all the next day.

The sun's beating down on my back so hot I feel like I'll burn up. Mama used to say she could tolerate the cold better than the heat because she could put on another sweater but couldn't peel off her skin. Heat waves are shimmering off the asphalt in the street. Suddenly I feel the fish come up in my throat. I sit back and close my eyes.

"Better take a break," Mr. Willie says, getting me the thermos and pouring some water into the cup. "It's frying hot today."

I take a small sip and wait for a minute. "What do you think we ought to plant?" I ask.

"Radishes," Mr. Willie says. "Big red ones."

"And carrots," I say, "the sweet kind, short and fat."

"Beans do well around here," Mr. Willie says.

"And cucumbers," I say, getting back to work.

Me and Mama picked them small for pickling. Not vinegar pickles like most people make. Salt pickles, that's what they were. You put the cucumbers into a jar, then the water, then the salt, some dill, and a piece of rye bread on top because of the yeast.

Mr. Willie's shovel hits something hard. I get the railroad spike and start digging for Bach or Brahms, but there's just a plain old ugly rock under there.

"Better stop looking, Jerome," Mr. Willie says.

9

I lie down on the bed with Monte, but I can't fall asleep there with him breathing on one side of me and Damon close on the other.

I look over at the clock. Five minutes past four in the morning. I hear Uncle James in the shower. He goes down the back stairs and out to the car to go to work. It would be strange to go to work at night when everyone else is sleeping. Monte says he works double shifts because then he gets paid extra.

Monte moves his feet on the bed the way he does. That boy can't stay still, even when he's asleep. Maybe that's why he stays so small and skinny. His face looks younger too, especially with his eyes closed. You'd never guess he was going on ten.

I tiptoe over to the window. The sky's mostly dark, but you can tell morning is coming. Mama liked the morning too, before the sun, before the heat of the day. Even on school days sometimes we got up early to play our duets before the day really got started. David would stand at the door and wait for me so we could walk to school together. *Can you teach me to play piano?* he asked. Next year David will go to Brown Middle School, but on this side of Vine Street everyone has to go to Maplewood. By the time we're together again in high school, I might not even recognize him.

I move my fingers on the windowsill like they're on a keyboard. I wonder who has our old piano now. Aunt Geneva said they had an estate sale. Said she didn't want me going just to see people buying our old stuff. When I asked if we could keep the piano, she shook her head. *We need the money, Jerome*, she said. *Raising kids does not come cheap. Soon as we can, Jerome, we'll buy a new piano, a shiny black one, okay? And we'll get lessons for you boys, that's what we'll do. Would you like that, Jerome?* I didn't answer because Mama was my teacher and Aunt Geneva had no business selling our piano that wasn't even hers.

I slip on my shorts, T-shirt, and shoes, and make my way down the stairs and out the front door. The air is warm and damp. Even in the dark I can see the old mansion. Mr. Willie's piano might still be inside somewhere.

I walk up to where the door used to be. To the right is a small window near the ground, filled with glass blocks. I pull at one of the blocks. It's loose. Slowly I work it out with my fingertips, and set it on the ground. The one next to it is loose too, but all the rest are in there solid. I'm too big to fit through that small hole. I crouch down, cup my hands around my eyes, and look inside. Dressers and boxes, doors and screens. The piano could be in the back somewhere. It's too dark to see. There's a noise in the bushes behind me. I hold my breath. Could be a cat. Or a raccoon. There are lots of raccoons around. They used to come into our garden at night and steal our tomatoes. I put the glass blocks back as quietly as I can.

I cross the gravel parking lot to the carriage house. Mr. Willie is probably sound asleep in there. I can knock on the door and say *Please, can I stay with you now that my mother passed? I don't like sleeping in a crowded room with boys breathing next to me.* I bet we can find a mattress somewhere. That's all I need. A mattress and a plain white sheet. I tap lightly on the board across the doorway and wait. The only sound is a faraway train.

What if Aunt Geneva wakes up and I'm gone? She'll search the house. She'll yell at Damon and Monte about how they treated me bad when it's not even true. She'll cry and say that her sister entrusted me to her, and now look what happened. *Jerome never causes any trouble*, Mama used to say. *You can count on Jerome for that.*

I walk slowly down the hill and go in through the front door. When I get to our room, both the boys are still in their beds with their eyes closed. I lie down next to Monte and wait for the sun to come up.

# 10

Mr. Willie is sorting stones into piles, big, medium, and small. "We'll extend the wall over to this side." He stands back. "It'll look better that way, don't you think?" He fills the bucket with new cement.

"Who taught you how to build walls?" I ask.

"Some things you learn by doing," Mr. Willie says.

I'm extending our garden toward the woods. Twice the shovel hits something and I think *Okay, this has to be Bach,* but both times it's just rocks.

A big white car pulls up the driveway and slows down in front of the For Sale sign. The people stay in the car, looking at the boarded-up mansion.

"What if they buy it?" I ask.

"Then it's sold," Mr. Willie says.

"But where will you stay after that?"

"You've asked me that before," Mr. Willie says. He bends over, picks up a stone, considers, tosses it into the small pile.

"You have to make plans," I say. "That's what my mother said. 'You can't blow with the wind, Jerome.'"

"I know that's right," Mr. Willie says. He stands up straight for a minute. "But things don't always go the way you think they will. In fact, most times they go the other way."

The white car pulls up a little, then stops again.

"Mama planned on me being a musician," I say.

"My mother had the same plan for me. Miss Myrtle too. She's the one who paid my tuition and got me the best piano teacher in the state of Ohio. In the whole country, I'm guessing." He pulls his eyebrows together. "Just some other things got in the way." He puts a glob of cement onto the wall.

"Other things like what?"

Mr. Willie sets a stone in place. "Like the color of my skin. Same color as yours." He smoothes the cement and some falls to the ground.

I know about all that, like Rosa Parks and Martin Luther King. I know the whole *I Have a Dream* speech from beginning to end. Me and Mama used to say it together, just the two of us, getting louder and louder, shouting out those words to nobody.

Mr. Willie puts the bucket down. "But then I made some mistakes too, that's for sure." Mr. Willie shakes his head. "Maybe I'm just looking for excuses." He tosses a small stone out of the way. "What I'm trying to say is that plans are fine, but—" Mr. Willie shrugs. "You never know the future, that's for sure."

The car takes off down the driveway.

Tears come to my eyes, but I'm not really crying. It's thinking about plans that gets me started. I wanted to stay right where I was with Mama when she had all her hair, sometimes in braids and sometimes in a bun on the top of her head. We each had our own room, and we had a kitchen and a living room with the piano. When I fell asleep at night, Mama would play me that Brahms lullaby. Just once I remember my daddy there, singing in a deep voice, because he had music in him too. "I didn't plan on my daddy leaving," I say.

Mr. Willie puts a rock in place. "I know that's right."

"Or my mother passing."

Mr. Willie nods.

"I planned on having a piano the rest of my life."

"Your life's not over yet," Mr. Willie says, straightening out his back. "And mine's not either."

# 11

We divide into two teams, me, Monte, Patrice, and Sandra on one, Damon, Ashley, Marc, and Wesley on the other. We have to find the flag and take it back across no-man's-land without getting put in jail.

"Where's jail?"

"The carriage house," Damon says.

I want to say *Did you ask Mr. Willie if you could use his place,* but Mr. Willie might not want the whole street to know where he stays.

Patrice assigns each of us a certain territory. "Yours is by the garage," she says, pointing to the garbage cans across the street.

It's late but not dark yet. Some of the garbage can lids are off. I bet they put the flag in there, in all those rotten banana peels and chicken bones and nasty stuff. I peek inside the first one and gag. No flag there. I look in the other two. Not there either.

Then in the half dark I see it in the sewer, that white rag with the corner sticking out. I look around. Nobody's near. I pull it out all wet and smelly. Then I'm running fast across no man's land with Damon on my tail, grabbing my shirt. I'm fat but I'm fast. I twist and run, he grabs my shirt again, and this time I feel his nails on my skin, but too late, I'm over the line, trying so hard to breathe, just to get the air. I'm coughing bad but the flag is ours.

Monte pats me on the back. "We did it, Jerome, we won." He's jumping and giving high fives to me and Sandra. "You're our man, Jerome."

"You're on our team tomorrow," Damon says.

"He is not," Monte says.

"He is so."

Finally I catch my breath. "I don't know if I'm playing tomorrow," I say.

"What plans you got?" Damon asks.

I shrug.

"I asked you a question." Damon is in my face, his fists clenched, dancing around. "You digging up dead people over there with that bum friend of yours? You talking to the ghosts?"

"Least I got something worth doing."

"Like what?"

"We're fixing a stone wall and making a garden."

"'We're fixing a stone wall and making a garden.'" He mimics my voice that is higher than his. "And where were you the other night, I'd like to know."

"What night?"

"You know what I'm talking about, so stop acting like you don't."

Could Damon have seen me taking out those glass blocks? The other kids are standing around, making a circle like they do on the playground when a fight is about to start. Mama always said *I'm lucky with you, Jerome, because you stay far from trouble.* But Mama's gone now and I have to decide for myself. I feel Damon's fist on my shoulder, not hard really, just firm.

"I saw you out there, trying to break in," Damon says.

"I was not."

"What were you doing then, hanging around out here in the middle of the night?"

I punch Damon in his stomach so hard he folds up like a lawn chair, folds and then unfolds, pulls his arm back. Then I feel somebody's arms around me, holding me down. I twist to get free, but he's stronger than I am and he won't let go. "Take it easy now, Jerome." The voice is Mr. Willie's.

"He started it," I say.

"Doesn't matter," Mr. Willie says.

I twist again, but Mr. Willie's arms are like ropes around my shoulders, pinning my arms to my sides. "Why don't you hold him?" I say, moving my chin toward Damon.

"He is not my business," Mr. Willie whispers.

"I'm not either," I say. I want to call the words back, but it's too late.

Slowly Mr. Willie loosens his grip. "Game's over," he says to all of us.

"We could call the police on you," Damon says to Mr. Willie. He motions toward the carriage house. "You aren't allowed to just start living somewhere," he says. "It's against the law."

Sandra shrugs. "You sound like a lawyer or something." She turns to her sister. "Let's go."

I take a deep breath and let it out slow. All those years the boys at school teased me because I play the piano and I talk proper and I'm fat, and all those years I never once got into a fight. Mama said *You know who you are in your heart, Jerome. All that's just words.* But now it seems like I forgot everything Mama ever taught me. I'm crying in the dark and Mr. Willie lets me go.

"Time to come in, boys," Aunt Geneva calls from the porch.

Mr. Willie's already heading back up the street. I want to run after him and say *I'm sorry for what I said. Can I please stay with you? We'll find a piano somewhere for sure and start practicing a duet just like you used to play with Sharon. I only need a mattress, that's all.*

Monte puts his hand on my arm. "Come on."

Damon is already up ahead. I don't want to go to Aunt Geneva's and sleep in the room with Damon. I want to go to my own house with my own piano.

Monte is pulling me toward the porch light.

# 12

"Is something the matter?" Aunt Geneva asks soon as she sees me.

"He's a crybaby," Damon says.

"Now you just stay quiet," Miss Geneva says to Damon, holding me close. "Are you okay? I thought I heard something going on out there." She gets me a damp washcloth to wipe my face. Then she says, "Was it Damon bothering you again?"

I don't answer.

She turns to Damon. "Next time there's trouble, I'm telling Daddy."

"Go ahead," Damon says.

"Stop it right there," Aunt Geneva says, her voice so deep you can hardly hear it.

"He started it," Damon says. "You can ask anyone. He punched me first."

"Not one more word, you hear?" Aunt Geneva's voice is shaking. "Jerome is not a fighting boy, you know that."

She is holding my arm. I want to tell her it's true, I did punch first. I wasn't a fighting boy before, but I am now. People don't stay the same forever. But the words are stuck in my throat.

"I want you to apologize," Aunt Geneva says to Damon.

Damon looks down. Aunt Geneva sighs. "He's just going through a stage. Best thing is not to pay any attention to it." She puts her arm around me. "Now I want you boys to go look in your room. I have a surprise for you."

There are three beds in our room and new polka-dotted sheets on each one. "How do you like it?" Aunt Geneva asks, following us up the stairs.

"Thank you," I say.

"Thanks," Monte says.

Damon is quiet.

Aunt Geneva pulls me close. "I have three boys now," she says. "Did you know I always wanted three children? James said two was more than enough, but now I got my way."

Aunt Geneva smells like soap, not the lemon soap that Mama used, but soap so strong it stings your eyes. I try to scoot away but her arm is heavy on my shoulder. Damon looks at his mom like *Sure, you wanted three boys, but did you ever ask me?* I want to tell him nobody asked me either, but he's turned the other way.

Monte takes the bed by the wall, I take the middle, and Damon takes the end. We lie there not moving and not talking. After a while I can tell from their breathing that they are asleep, but those dots on the sheets are like eyeballs all around. Mama's eyes were gray before she passed, cloudy-like. *That's not the cancer*, she said, *that's cataracts.*

I bury my face into the pillow that smells like the candy in a department store. Aunt Geneva said our house sold quick, but she didn't say who bought it. I asked *Can we go back and see who's there?* She said *No use in that, Jerome.* And I said *But I want to visit my friend David who lives across the street,* and she said *Not yet, Jerome, let time go by.* I asked *How much time?* and she said *We'll see, Jerome, how things are going.*

Could be whoever bought the house bought my bed too, with the pale blue sheets. Could be another boy is sleeping there now. Maybe he went across the street to play with David. Or maybe he has brothers and sisters of his own.

I sit up and move my fingers on the mattress, right hand harder, left hand soft, Sonata in G Major by Scarlatti. Mom loved that one, the way I played it loud, over the sound of the oxygen.

"Jerome." Monte's voice is loud. "What are you doing?"

"Nothing."

"How come you're sitting up?" He scoots over to my mattress. I wish he'd just go back to sleep so I could keep on with the Scarlatti. "You're not leaving, are you?" he says.

I shrug. "No place to go."

He looks at his sleeping brother. "Damon didn't mean anything. He gets mad all the time." Monte shivers even though it's hot in the room.

"You better go back to sleep," I whisper.

"You're not leaving, are you?" he repeats.

"You just asked me that."

"I know. I was wondering."

"I told you to go to sleep." My voice is hard.

"I'm trying. But I can't." Then Monte is crying.

"Stop or you'll wake Damon up."

He's trying, but the sobs keep coming. Monte doesn't have a thing to cry about. He has his mom, his dad, his brother, when I don't have anyone. *Pity doesn't go too far, Jerome*, Mama said, *and you have a tendency to mull.*

Finally Monte swallows hard and looks toward the window. "I can't believe you found that marble head out there."

"Mr. Willie found it."

"Now what are you digging for?"

"Just making a garden."

Damon turns over on the bed and I think we're talking too loud.

"Can I help you?" Monte's voice is begging.

Monte is leaning against me. We hear the screech of a catfight somewhere behind the house. Then Uncle James's car pulls in.

"I miss your mama too," Monte says suddenly.

"You do?" I never thought of that.

"I used to wish I could stay at your house."

"Why's that?"

Monte looks over at his brother. "Your mother said

when I got older, she'd teach me how to play piano just like you."

"I'll teach you," I say.

"We don't have a piano."

"Your mom said we're getting one."

"And then you can teach me," he says, lying down on my mattress. Soon his breathing is slow and even. There's a breeze blowing in through the open window. I cover Monte with the sheet.

# 13

Mr. Willie cleans Ms. Smith's garage, and she gives him a whole bag of seeds in small envelopes: beans, cucumbers, lettuce, spinach, carrots, tomatoes, radishes.

"Why don't people pay you with money?" I ask.

"They do, sometimes. But trading is simpler. More basic. I used to trade piano playing for haircuts, food, whatever."

"Mama did that sometimes, like she cooked a chicken for the lady who tuned our piano."

"Tuning is something I never could do," Mr. Willie says.

Mama said *Can you hum a C, Jerome*, and I closed my eyes and the C came out low and clear. *That boy has perfect pitch*, she told Daddy, *isn't that a gift?* Daddy said *What's that good for? So he can tune pianos the rest of his life?*

"My mother said I have perfect pitch," I say.

"Now that's a stroke of luck," Mr. Willie says. "Sharon had it too, even with her hearing as bad as it was."

I keep on digging, turning over the soil, breaking up the clods. "Where is Sharon now?"

"Last I heard, she was staying down on Reading Road," Mr. Willie says. "In one of those group homes."

I pick up a fat worm and watch it wriggle in my

palm. "After Sharon left, did Miss Myrtle still teach you piano?"

Mr. Willie nods. "Every day. She got me ready for my audition."

"Audition?"

"You had to audition to get into the music conservatory."

"And you got in?"

Mr. Willie nods. "I was so nervous I could hardly stop shaking and I thought nobody can play the piano shaking like a leaf, but once I got past the first measure, I forgot all about the audition because the music was in me and it was coming out."

"What were you playing?"

"Bach Invention Number Eleven in G Minor."

"Me and Mama were working on those inventions."

"They look simple but they're hard to play. Each hand is separate, doing its own thing, but then they come back together."

"It's like being with someone even when you're not," I say.

Mama played the left hand and I played the right, not too loud. Sometimes we got our hands all tangled up. *Our fingers are like spaghetti*, she said, laughing. When she got sick I played both hands, making the melody come out louder so she could hear the tune. She closed her eyes and listened, and I heard her breathe and thought *What if she just stops?*

"We'll play those inventions someday," Mr. Willie says.

# 14

We have lunch inside the carriage house. Mr. Willie brings out a loaf of bread, peanut butter, and jelly. He makes three sandwiches, one for him, one for me, and one to share. I'm looking around Mr. Willie's place. The floor is broken-up concrete. There's a mattress in one corner, a few hooks with shirts, and a wooden shelf with Mr. Beethoven on top.

"Hey, Jerome." Monte's voice is close, coming from outside. "Hey, Jerome, where are you?"

I go out, holding my sandwich. "What do you want?"

"Look." Monte points to a big white Cadillac parked right in front of the mansion. Three white men in suits get out of the car. They walk up the front steps, but they don't go in. Then they come around back and look at the carriage house and at me and Monte. They poke around for a few minutes in the honeysuckle bushes. Finally they get back into their Cadillac and drive back down the way they came.

Mr. Willie comes out with a thermos. "Someone was looking at the mansion," I say.

"Looking isn't buying," he says.

"They might buy it," I say.

"Might or might not. No matter. We got our work to do," he says, reaching for the bucket.

"Can I help?" Monte asks.

I wish he wouldn't follow me around, but Mr. Willie says, "I can use all the help I can get." Then he tells Monte what size stone he needs, small, medium, or large, and Monte gets it for him.

"Mama and Ms. Smith and Ms. Jackson were talking, and they said whoever buys this place is most definitely taking it down," Monte says.

"You mean the carriage house?"

"I mean everything," Monte says.

We don't need to hear what's going to happen when Monte has no idea what he's talking about. I didn't need to hear either, how Mama's hair was going to fall out and she was going to get weaker and weaker. Anyway it wasn't true because she dug carrots in our garden the day before she passed. She said *Jerome, don't forget to dig the potatoes out small. New potatoes are better than old ones, you know.*

Mr. Willie's working fast, not talking, building that wall up like it was new. I'm using the leftover rocks to divide our garden into four sections.

The Cadillac comes back around. The men are sitting inside with the windows up and the air conditioner on. The driver rolls his window down. "You know anything about this place?" he asks.

"A little," Mr. Willie says.

"Looks like it's been abandoned for quite some time," he says.

"Several years," Mr. Willie says.

The man stretches his neck out the window. "The neighborhood seems a bit rundown."

Mr. Willie looks that man right in his eyes. "Depends on how you look at it."

The man drives off without thanking us.

Damon is there, bouncing his basketball. "What they want?" he asks his brother.

"They said the neighborhood is rundown."

Damon laughs. "Like we need them to tell us." He moves the basketball around his waist, then pretends to make a shot. "What you digging for now?" he asks.

I don't answer.

"You deaf or something?"

"We're fixing the wall and making a garden," I say.

"Farmers." He laughs. "Couple of farmers, that's what you are. Mama's looking for you," he says to his brother.

"What for?"

"You better go find out."

Monte and Damon disappear down the hill.

Mr. Willie stoops to pick up a small rock and cleans it off on his jeans. "Well, if this isn't special," he says, handing it to me. "Know what it is?"

The stone is chiseled and triangular. "An arrowhead?" I ask.

Mr. Willie nods. "A little piece of history. You know, long before they built this mansion, there was forest here, and the Indians hunted dear, turkey, wild boar." Mr. Willie sets a stone in place. "Like I told you, there's history in everything."

I breathe on the arrowhead and shine it with my T-shirt. It looks brand-new, like it was made yesterday instead of a few hundred years ago.

"Keep it," Mr. Willie says.

I put the arrowhead into my pocket to show to Mama. No, Mama's not at home waiting for me, waiting to hear about my day, waiting to see what's in my pockets. *That's a buffalo-head nickel, Jerome. You found it on the sidewalk? You have good eyes, like I used to when I was a girl. Let's go to the library, Jerome, and find a book about coins so we can start a collection.*

Mr. Willie gets the thermos and pours us each a cup of cold water. We drink it fast. He starts humming a tune as he rinses our cups in the hose.

"The first movement of the Mozart Piano Concerto no. 23," I say.

Mr. Willie looks way down the street. "The day I got into the conservatory, Miss Myrtle was so happy she couldn't stop crying." Mr. Willie shakes his head. "Only thing she didn't consider was that being a black piano player wasn't going to be so easy."

"Why not?"

Mr. Willie straightens out his back. "People always

assumed I was serving food at the gigs, not playing piano." He looks down. "One time they told me to go in the back door, and I said I am part of a quintet, sir, I am the pianist."

Mr. Willie saying that makes me feel funny, like all that history Mama told me about wasn't really so long ago after all, like if it could happen to Mr. Willie it could happen to me too.

"Excuses. Maybe I'm just making up excuses," Mr. Willie says.

"For what?"

"For why I didn't finish at the conservatory."

"Do you think you'll be playing the piano again?"

"No doubt," Mr. Willie says.

"Was it a grand you used to play?"

"Upright," Mr. Willie says. "A big white upright."

"Mine was black," I say.

# 15

Mr. Willie gets a longer garden hose from Ms. Sullivan in return for fixing her back steps. He screws it onto the other hose so we can water the garden, since we don't seem to be getting any rain these days and it's been over ninety degrees for more than two weeks straight. The TV calls it an inversion layer. Aunt Geneva says they can call it whatever they want, but, fact is, we are baking to a crisp in Cincinnati.

I'm spraying the little radish plants when a half-falling-apart van pulls up in front of the mansion. A couple gets out, a man with silver hair past his shoulders and a skinny little lady who smiles at me. She takes a crowbar out of the van and hands it to the man. He hands it back. Then she goes to the front door of the mansion and tries to pry the board off, but it's nailed pretty tight. Finally the man helps her and they go on in.

"They're breaking into Miss Myrtle's house," Mr. Willie says. "Right in front of me, just breaking in." He looks down the hill. "She would be most unhappy about that."

We watch for a while, but the man and the lady don't come out. I'm making the paths around the garden out of the stones Mr. Willie doesn't need for the wall. Monte's helping me, sorting rocks, mostly. He's finding fossils too, like brachiopods and bryozoans.

"These must be more than one hundred years old," Monte says.

"You mean one thousand," I say.

"You mean more than five hundred million," Mr. Willie says.

Hearing those numbers makes me feel small, like we're just a tiny speck in the universe. Mama used to say *Jerome, we got to do the best we can for the short time we're on this earth,* and I said *It's not short because a day has twenty-four hours and there's seven days in a week and fifty-two weeks in a year, so if you multiply all that there's eight thousand seven hundred thirty-six hours in a year, and that's a lot of time.* Mama said *Not as long as you think, in the scheme of things.* I wonder how long Mama had cancer before we even knew.

The man comes out with the lady behind him. "Is this a safe neighborhood?" the lady asks.

"There's no trouble around here," Mr. Willie says.

Then the man points to the carriage house. "Condemned buildings like this aren't good for a neighborhood." He talks to the lady like we aren't even there.

"Maybe we can fix it up," she says. "It's an interesting structure."

The man shakes his head. "Too far gone."

They head back to the van. "See you around." The lady smiles and waves to us.

"What's 'condemned' mean?" I ask Mr. Willie.

"The building has to be fixed up."

"What if it's not?"

He makes a flat motion with his hand.

*Too far gone*, the man said. *Gone too far.* That's what the doctor said. If it was sooner, maybe they could have done something, but the cancer had gone too far, spread all over, like poison ivy in Aunt Geneva's yard.

# 16

Aunt Melinda is visiting from New York. Aunt Geneva has us cleaning every corner of the house. I scrub the bathroom and Monte vacuums the rugs. Damon's supposed to be washing the floors, but Miss Geneva says he's sloshing water all over and just moving the dirt around. "Don't you know how to clean better than that?"

"First you tell me to clean and then you tell me I can't do it right." He throws the sponge into the bucket.

"You better not talk to me like that," Aunt Geneva says. She looks at me. "Now I know your mother never put up with that kind of talk."

I swallow hard. Once Mama tried to help me tuck in my shirt and I said *Leave me alone,* and she said *Jerome, I never talk to you that way and I don't expect you to talk to me that way either.*

"Get on your knees and finish this floor," Aunt Geneva says to Damon.

He's breathing deep, just standing there. I want to say *You better get on all fours and at least look like you're cleaning.*

"You heard me," Aunt Geneva says.

Damon kicks the side of the bucket, spilling out

some water, then runs down the stairs. We hear the front door slam shut.

Monte is vacuuming the rugs over and over even though they're already clean. I know he's afraid to stop, afraid of how mad Miss Geneva might be. She turns the volume on the radio up real high, then takes the sponge out of the bucket, squeezes out the excess water, and starts cleaning the floor herself and mumbling all kinds of things about what she's going to do when Damon comes back.

"You never talked back like that, did you, Jerome." Aunt Geneva is emptying the bucket into the toilet. "And to think that she raised you by herself." Aunt Geneva shakes her head.

I'm scrubbing the bathtub and the tile around the faucets. I told Mama I wasn't going to scrub the toilet because it was nasty, and she said *Are you going to leave the nasty work for your mother? Is that what you have in mind?*

Aunt Melinda has a bag of clothes her son outgrew. She dumps them on the clean rug and says, "Now you boys see what fits who. No sense buying new clothes when you'll outgrow them before the year is out."

I want to go see Mr. Willie, but Aunt Melinda says, "Go on, try them on."

"Now?" Monte asks.

"No time like the present," Aunt Geneva says, handing him a small button-down shirt.

"That's a size seven," Aunt Melinda says.

"Monte's not much bigger than a seven-year-old," Aunt Geneva says, and sure enough, it fits just right.

"Where is Damon?" Aunt Melinda asks.

"He stomped off somewhere," Aunt Geneva says.

Aunt Melinda shakes her head. "It's hard to raise boys right anymore."

"Sy didn't seem to have a problem." Aunt Geneva puts her arm around me.

Sy. Most people called Mama Sylvia, all except for her two older sisters. They said when Mama was a baby she couldn't pronounce Sylvia, so they shortened it to Sy, even though that sounds more like a man's name to me. My daddy called her Sy too, that's what I remember. *Sy, sit over here by me. Okay, Sy?*

Aunt Melinda hands me a flannel shirt. It's so hot but I still have to try it on. "Too tight under the arms," she says. She hands me a T-shirt that says Broncos on the front. I pull it over my head and she straightens out the front. "Not bad," she says.

"Now can I go out?" I ask.

"It's time for lunch," Aunt Geneva says.

After Aunt Melinda leaves to visit a friend, we have to clean up. Then Uncle James comes home and we have an early supper. I'm so tired of being in this house, but it doesn't seem like I'll have any chance to find Mr. Willie.

"Where's Damon?" Uncle James asks.

"We had a little altercation," Aunt Geneva says.

"Is that right?" Uncle James looks out the window. "He may have another not-so-little altercation when he gets home."

After dinner, Uncle James takes a quick nap before getting up for his shift. By the time me and Monte do the dishes, the sun is almost set. There's a bit of leftover chili in the pot.

"Can I take it to Mr. Willie?" I ask.

Aunt Geneva considers. I know she's thinking *What about saving some for Damon,* but then she puts all of it into an empty cottage-cheese container and says, "Sure, Mr. Willie could use some meat on his bones."

I knock on the door, but Mr. Willie isn't home. I go inside and wait for my eyes to adjust to the darkness. Everything is in order, the way Mr. Willie likes it, his mattress with the sheet pulled smooth, his shirt on a hook, the shelf with Mr. Beethoven. Something rustles in the corner. A squirrel maybe, or a mouse. Damon says this place is haunted, but Mama said there's no such thing as ghosts. *What about when someone dies?* I asked. *Then they are part of the soil,* she said. *What about fossils,* I said. *They come from dead things and they aren't part of the soil.* Mama said *You have a point there, Jerome.* Maybe someday Mama's bones will be fossils so I can keep them forever.

I leave the chili in the middle of the table for Mr. Willie.

# 17

When we go to bed, Damon is still not home.

"What if he never comes back?" Monte asks.

"He'll be back soon as he's hungry," I say.

Monte's sniffling and rubbing his eyes.

"Stop it," I say. "He'll be back."

"He'll get hisself into trouble."

"What trouble?"

"He always gets into some kind of trouble." Monte's trying not to cry. "Daddy's going to beat him when he gets home." Monte has his face in the pillow, muffling his voice. "I told him not to get into trouble all the time. I told him."

Our room is stuffy and my chest feels tight. I go over to the window and raise it as far as it will go. There's a slight breeze blowing like it might finally rain. But it could just as well pass us by. I move my fingers on the windowsill, playing an old tune that I know from I don't know where.

Monte is there, his hand on my shoulder, looking out the window. "Where do you think Damon went?"

"Probably just hanging around somewhere."

"By hisself?"

"With his friends."

"He doesn't have any friends," Monte says. "Nobody much gets along with Damon."

"You do," I say. "And the kids in the neighborhood."

"Not really." His voice is squeaky. "Not anymore. Ashley and Marc told me they're not hanging with Damon anymore. Wesley either."

"Why not?"

Monte's rubbing his eyes and I think we better talk about something else.

"It might rain," I say.

"You think it stays dry in Mr. Willie's when it rains?" Monte asks.

"Mostly."

"You think Mr. Willie likes staying over there?" Monte points up the hill.

"I don't know."

"Do you like staying here?" Monte asks.

"Like it or not, doesn't matter." I liked it in my old house with our piano in the living room and David across the street.

"But do you?" His grip is tight on my shoulder, his fingernails digging into my skin. I know what he wants me to say, but I'm not ready to say it.

"You're hurting me," I say, twisting away.

He drops his hand.

# 18

Monte crawls onto my bed and falls asleep. Hard to believe he's nine, the way he's afraid of everything.

I'm seeing all those polka dots like eyeballs again. I close my eyes for what seems like hours, but sleep still won't come. Why was it my mama who got cancer? Why wasn't it somebody who smoked cigarettes all day long, somebody who deserved it? Mama said *Nobody deserves illness, Jerome, nobody.* Even if they smoke? *Even then.* My chest is feeling tight every day now, like the air's too thick. *Concentrate on each breath,* Mama said, *one, two, three, like Beethoven's Moonlight Sonata, the first movement, slow and steady.* I need a piano so bad. I need to move my fingers on the keys and hear the sound and know it's me that's making that music, nobody else but me.

I put on my shorts and shoes, and go down the steps to the basement. There must be something down here I can use to take out more of those glass blocks. Uncle James has his tools hanging neatly on a pegboard. There's a whole set of screwdrivers. I take the biggest one off the board and stick it into my back pocket. Then I go quietly up the stairs and out the front door. If I can just pry out two more glass blocks then I can fit inside. I bet Sharon's piano is back there somewhere. I bet it is.

Damon is crouched under a street lamp smoking. His back is to me, but I know it's him by the hunched shoulders and the long arms. I duck behind the garbage cans and watch. Another kid walks up and they whisper together. It's a boy even taller than he is who I've never seen before. Damon helps him light a cigarette. I see the orange light and then white smoke. They are standing close, whispering I think, and reaching in their pockets. After a minute, Damon heads one way down the street and his friend goes the other.

With the screwdriver, I can get one more glass block out, but the rest are rock solid, and the hole isn't near big enough for me to fit through. I try to put the tip of the screwdriver into the small crack between the blocks, but when I push down, the metal bends. I try to bend it back and the screwdriver turns in my grip. Uncle James will be so mad. He's particular about his tools.

A car moves slowly down the street. Maybe somebody heard me and called the police. Breaking and entering. *Jerome stays far from trouble*, Mama told Aunt Geneva. She rubbed my head with her dry palms. *Yes, I'm lucky with that boy, I sure am.* Aunt Geneva said *It's not all luck.* And Mama said *There's luck in it too, you know.*

I hear footsteps behind me and whip my head around. There is Monte, in his pajamas and bare feet. "What are you doing here?" I ask him.

He puts his hands up like he's protecting his face or

something. "You weren't in the bed." Monte looks down. "I was scared in the room by myself."

I want to tell him not to act like a baby, but I stop myself when I see he's shaking like a leaf.

"What are you doing?" he asks, coming closer.

"Nothing much."

Monte sees the three glass blocks on the ground and the hole where they were. "You trying to get in there?"

"Yup."

"What for?"

"I'm looking for a piano."

"In this old house?"

"Mr. Willie said they used to have a white piano."

Monte looks at the hole and the glass blocks on the ground. "I can fit through," he whispers.

I look at his skinny shoulders. I bet he really can get himself through. He sticks his head into the hole, wriggles his shoulders, then scoots so only his legs are out. "It's dark in here, Jerome."

"Wait a minute and let your eyes get used to it," I whisper.

He stays like that, half in and half out. Then he starts wriggling his hips through the opening until finally he is inside.

"You see anything?"

He doesn't answer.

I cup my hands around my eyes and peek in. "What do you see?" I ask.

"Boxes. Lots of boxes and stuff."

"Look for a piano."

"I'm looking. But I don't see one."

"You have to walk around. It's big. And white."

"I know. I still don't see one."

Monte moves forward, then stops. "What was that?"

"What?"

"That noise."

"There's no noise. Keep looking."

"There's no piano that I can see."

"How about in the basement?"

"I'm scared to go down there by myself," Monte says.

"Hurry. Just take a quick look."

Monte moves forward, then turns back. "I'm scared, Jerome. Can I come out now?" He's wriggling his way out just as fast as he can. His pajama shirt gets caught on something and tears, but he's in such a hurry he doesn't care. Finally he's next to me, holding onto my arm, trembling. "It's haunted in there," he says. "It's a haunted house."

"There's no such thing as a haunted house," I say, taking his hand.

"Damon says there is."

I grab his arm. "There isn't. My mother said."

Monte looks into the dark hole where the glass block was. "Later I'll look in the basement. I promise."

I put the glass block back in place. "Come on," I say to Monte, pulling him down the hill.

I take the screwdriver back to the basement and hang it on the pegboard. Maybe Uncle James won't notice that it's bent. In the corner is a crowbar. Next time I'll use that and make the hole big enough so I can fit inside and find that piano myself. Then I'll start fixing up the front room, cleaning out the spiderwebs and washing down the walls. *The floor is the last part to clean,* Mama said. *Work your way toward the door or you'll clean yourself into a corner, Jerome.*

# 19

Mr. Willie has a lot of work to do before fall. He's painting Mr. Loman's porch and fixing Ms. Alonzo's windows. Then there's lots of raking and sweeping and planting bulbs all over the place. I take care of our garden, and Monte follows me everywhere, chattering the whole time.

"How come you plant the cucumbers in little hills? How come the beans are all bent over like that? Who taught you how to play the piano? When can you start teaching me?"

Sometimes I stop answering and he says, "Jerome, are you mad?"

Damon's been going out almost every night after dinner. Sometimes he comes home late at night and sometimes he doesn't come home at all. Uncle James took off his belt the other day, getting ready to whip that boy, but Aunt Geneva said, "A boy that big is too old to be whipped." Uncle James said, "Then he's too old to be staying under this roof," and Aunt Geneva got all teary-eyed. She used to ask did we know where he was, but since we never did, she stopped asking. Sometimes I see her gazing up the street and I see sadness in her eyes like how Mama looked when Daddy stopped coming around. First he had to go out of town on business for a day or two, then a whole week. I always pushed a chair to the window so I could wait for his car to turn the corner. *It's late, Jerome, time for bed. No, I'm waiting for my daddy. Jerome, go to bed now. Will Daddy be here in the morning?* Mama sat at the piano and played the first movement of the Moonlight Sonata over and over into the night.

I go out early one morning before Monte wakes up and before the sun and head up the hill. The skinny lady is in front of the carriage house, poking around.

"You're up bright and early today," she says. "Looks like a nice garden you got there."

"Thank you."

She reaches into her bag. "I brought these for you," she says, handing me a plastic bag of black seeds.

"I already got most of the planting done," I say.

"These are flower seeds. Four o'clocks. They grow pretty much anywhere."

"Thank you, ma'am."

"Ginny," she says. "Call me Ginny. And this is Tom." She points to the silver-haired man. He's fixing the front door hinges.

Mr. Willie comes up the street and sees us.

"You're early today," he says to me.

"I'm Ginny," the lady says. "Ginny Bossard and Tom Owens." She reaches out to shake Mr. Willie's hand. "Your new neighbors."

I see Mr. Willie flinch. "Neighbors?"

"We signed yesterday," Ginny says. "Hey, Tom, come over here and meet our new neighbors. What did you say your name was?"

"Wilson."

"Pleased to meet you, Mr. Wilson."

"Wilson's the first name," Mr. Willie says.

Tom sets the drill down and stands by Ginny.

"I was just telling Wilson here and his friend—" Ginny looks at me.

"Jerome."

"—Jerome, that it's official."

"When are you moving in?" Mr. Willie asks.

"Moving in? Oh, we're not going to actually live here." She takes Tom's hand. "We're starting a school in September."

My breathing feels tight. Me and Mr. Willie need three rooms, one bedroom for each of us and a big room for our concerts.

"A school in this old house?" Mr. Willie asks.

"It's perfect," Ginny says. "We'll have the smaller children on the first floor, the bigger ones upstairs. We'll cook wholesome food in the kitchen." Her face moves as she talks and her hands too. "We got a government grant to get started."

"What grade is it up to?" I ask.

"We'll start with kindergarten and first, then add one more grade each year."

"I see," Mr. Willie says.

Ginny is waiting for him to say something else, but Mr. Willie is quiet. Tom goes back to his drilling. She takes some boxes out of the van. "We are in a real hurry to get at least the front room ready for the beginning of the school year," she says.

"What about the rest of the house?" I ask.

"That may have to wait," Ginny says.

"How long?"

"I'm not really sure," Ginny says. "First we'll have to see how it goes." That's what the doctor said. *See how it goes. You'll lose your hair after the second treatment.* For sure? *Nothing's ever sure, Mrs. Mason. That's what I've seen happen.*

Mr. Willie is starting across the street. "Where are you going?" I ask.

"I have some business to attend to," he says, heading toward the bus stop.

"Can I go with you?" I ask.

"Not today," Mr. Willie says firmly. He puts his hands in his pockets and turns the corner.

Ginny asks if I'd like to help.

"With what?" I ask.

"I was thinking you could help with the sanding," she says, "if it's okay with your mom."

I almost tell her that I can't ask my mom because she passed. Then Ginny will look at me like my teachers at school, whispering behind the door until I come close, saying *Poor boy, what's he going to do now?*

I want so bad to go into the old mansion, to search for the piano that must be there in one of those back rooms. "I'll ask," I say, running down the hill to Aunt Geneva's.

"If they're making a school out of that mess, I'm all for it," Aunt Geneva says. "Just be careful, Jerome. I don't want you using any power tools, saws, nothing like that. You hear?"

"Yes, ma'am."

# 20

Tom has taken off the boards so there's no door there, just a doorway. "Welcome," Ginny says, ushering me into Miss Myrtle's house. I can't believe I am actually inside. Everything is covered in a thick layer of dust. "It'll take some elbow grease, Jerome," she says, "But this is one beautiful building." She points to the staircase. "Marble," she says.

"Mr. Willie told me."

She looks at me sideways. "You mean Wilson?"

I nod.

"He told you that?"

"Yes, ma'am. He was a good friend of Sharon's. She used to live here a long time ago."

I start coughing from all the dust. Ginny hands me a mask to wear over my mouth and nose. "Here, this'll help a little," she says. Then she gives me a block of wood and a piece of sandpaper. "Have you ever sanded before?"

I shake my head. I'm not sure if I can talk with this mask on.

She wraps the wood with the sandpaper and moves it up and down on the wood floor. "Make sure to follow the grain," she says. She smoothes a spot. "See the lines, how they go this way? You have to sand with the grain or you'll scratch the wood."

"Yes, ma'am." My voice is muffled.

"No 'ma'am,'" she says.

"Yes, Miss Ginny."

"Just Ginny, okay?" Even with the mask over her mouth I can tell she's smiling by all the little lines around her eyes. "I'm going to work in the other room. You call me if you need anything, okay?"

I nod.

"Any questions?"

Suddenly there's something I have to know. "Is there a piano in here?"

"A piano, did you say?"

"Yes, ma'am, I mean Ginny."

"I haven't seen one," she says. "But that doesn't mean there isn't one in here somewhere. We haven't explored the half of it yet. Some of the back rooms are still locked."

"There used to be a piano," I say.

"I see."

"Mr. Willie used to play it. A while back."

"We'll keep an eye out for it," she says.

"There are some sculptures too. Bach and Brahms."

"Is that right? We'll look around."


I sand with the grain. *Busy hands heal a broken heart,* Mama said. *You don't see me sitting idle, do you, Jerome. You don't see me sitting around and waiting for things to happen.* The only place Mama ever sat for longer than a meal was on the piano bench.

I wipe away the dust with my palm. Mama had a smooth wooden bowl on the dresser that Daddy gave her for her birthday. When she was getting ready for work, I sat on the bed holding that bowl, feeling the inside and the outside as smooth as skin.

I stand up straight and look around. The ceiling is really high and there are designs carved into the woodwork. Me and Mr. Willie will put the grand piano in here. The chairs can go in a semicircle around the side of the room. Or maybe long straight rows would be better.

"Finished?"

I jump.

"I didn't mean to startle you," Ginny says, touching the wood floor where I sanded it. "Nice job. It looks professional." She hands me ten dollars. "Thank you, Jerry. You are a big help."

I put the money into my pocket. I'm not Jerry, I'm Jerome. Jerome William Mason. I'll show Mama I have a real job now. No, not Mama, not anyone. I'll save my money until I can buy my own piano. I'll look in the newspaper for an estate sale. People are dying all the time, and some of them have pianos to sell, I know that.

Mr. Willie is still not back. What if he decided to leave now that Ginny and Tom bought the mansion? Maybe he's already found some other place to stay. Maybe he won't even come back to say good-bye.

Business to attend to, he said. He didn't say work to do or a job on the other side of town. I stand in front of the carriage house and my breathing feels tight. Suddenly I have to know if Mr. Willie has already moved out.

I open the door. Beethoven is there on the small shelf. The bed is made. The container I brought the chili in is empty and washed. Mr. Willie's shirts are hanging on the hooks. I pull the door shut. He would tell me if he was leaving. I know he would.

I dig up the dirt around the carriage-house door and plant the four o'clock seeds all around.

# 21

Aunt Geneva tells me to put on a button-down shirt because we have an appointment with a lawyer.

"What appointment?" I ask.

"Hurry, Jerome." She hands me a light blue shirt that's too tight across my stomach. "The lawyer might charge us if we're late."

"Can I come?" Monte asks.

"We won't be long," Aunt Geneva shouts over her shoulder.

I look back, and Monte is standing in the doorway looking so small and skinny. Uncle James is asleep. Damon is who knows where. Aunt Geneva is hurrying me along. The bus pulls up just as we get to the stop, and we find two seats near the front.

Aunt Geneva puts her arm around my shoulders. Then she looks at her watch. "We should be just on time."

"Why are we going to a lawyer?"

"To help us make things legal."

I stiffen.

Aunt Geneva looks out the bus window. "You know, Jerome, you are a blessing to us. Monte smiles every time he looks at you."

"Not Damon," I say.

I can feel the sweat from her arm on my neck. "That has nothing to do with you."

"I don't know," I say.

Aunt Geneva sits up straight. "I don't want you thinking like that, Jerome. Damon was going his way long before you came to stay with us."

We're passing the fried-chicken place with a smell that makes my stomach queasy. Aunt Geneva takes some papers out of her purse. I see Mama's name on the top.

"What's that?" I ask.

"It shows the date that Sy—that your mama passed," she says.

"May twenty-eighth," I say.

"I know," Aunt Geneva says. "But they need an official record." She clicks the purse shut.

"Official record to know that Mama died?"

Aunt Geneva takes a deep breath. "We need it so that Uncle James and I can officially adopt you."

Adopt like at the animal shelter. Adopt a kitten. Adopt a puppy. Give it a home. Everything is going by so fast out the window, the White Castle and the Quik Stop and the playground. The bus jerks to a stop, then starts again, making my stomach come up to my throat. What if I throw up on this bus?

I push myself against the window where the air conditioning is coming out. "What if I don't want to be adopted?" I ask.

Aunt Geneva pushes back against the seat. I know she's thinking *I can't believe Jerome said that.* "It's what your mama wanted," she says.

I close my eyes. Did anybody ever ask me? *Just put on this shirt, Jerome. Hurry. We have an appointment with a lawyer.* "Mama never said a thing about anybody adopting me," I say.

"Shhh, Jerome. Your mother and I talked about it way back before she ever got sick. Before we had children even." Aunt Geneva takes a tissue out of her purse. "We promised to look after each other. And that includes you kids."

Tears are running down my face and snot too. Aunt Geneva offers me a tissue but I don't want it. I want to get off this bus and find Mr. Willie wherever he is. We'll play duets, that's what we'll do, in the front room of the big mansion. We'll play for money and sandwiches and peaches. Mr. Willie listens when I talk and says *I see your point, Jerome,* like Mama used to.

"If it's not legal, somebody could come along—you never know, Jerome," Aunt Geneva says. She is opening and shutting her purse, fiddling with the papers. I look out the dirty window. We are passing the City Garden Center. Me and Mama went there to get plants for our garden, some perennials for along the side of the house. Year after year they came back, getting so big we had to divide them. I start moving my fingers on the bus window. The right hand crosses over the left, back and forth, moving faster and faster. The bus stops at the corner and an old man gets on.

"I want Mr. Willie to adopt me," I say so loud that the

lady in front of us turns around.

Aunt Geneva acts like she doesn't hear. "Your mother was my sister," she whispers. She dabs at the tears on her cheeks.

I want Mama to be sitting here beside me. We could be heading downtown to the main library like we used to every Sunday. We could be picking out books and music and movies for the week. "I want a piano," I say finally.

"Someday, Jerome." Aunt Geneva takes another tissue out of her purse.

The bus pulls into the last stop at Government Square. We get off and cross the street to the courthouse. Inside are two marble staircases. We take the one on the left up to the second floor. "Room 201," Aunt Geneva says.

We have to wait a long time for our turn. People are coming and going. I could run fast down these stairs and out the door. But where would I go? Aunt Geneva asks me if I'm hungry.

"No, ma'am."

She hands me a peppermint anyway. "Helps the time pass," she says, unwrapping one and putting it into her mouth.

Mama liked mints too, the real hot ones that take your breath away.

When we finally see the lawyer, he says Aunt Geneva needs some other papers like her birth certificate and her marriage certificate to Uncle James. "Nobody told me to bring all that," Aunt Geneva says.

"Getting adopted is a process," the lawyer says. "We have to make sure everything is in order."

She makes another appointment for next week. The lawyer smiles at me with his big white teeth. "Don't worry," he says. "It'll all work out. We just have to take it step by step."

I want to tell him I'm not worried at all. It's not me that started this whole thing in the first place.

Aunt Geneva stands. "Thank you," she says, ushering me out into the hallway.

On the way home on the bus, Aunt Geneva falls asleep. With her eyes closed like that she looks a little like Mama. Same tall forehead and broad nose. But her mouth and chin are different.

Mama talked things over with me, big things and small things and everything in between. *Jerome, should I take that other job over in the nursing home or stick with what I have? Should we plant purple hostas on the side of the house or white ones? You're the one with the good eye, Jerome. Thank you, Jerome, you are a big help, you know that?*

The bus stops suddenly. Aunt Geneva opens her eyes for a minute, then closes them again. She never tells me a thing.

# 22

Monte is up by the carriage house. "Where were you?" he asks.

"Downtown."

"Doing what?"

"Visiting a lawyer."

"What for?"

I don't answer.

"That lady was here looking for you," Monte says.

"Ginny?"

"Skinny white lady," he says.

Maybe she came to tell me she found the piano in there, or the sculptures or something. I start running up toward the mansion.

"Can I go with you?" Monte asks.

"No." My voice is sharp.

"Why not?"

Monte is always following me everywhere, talking the whole time. What's he doing up here at Mr. Willie's place anyway? He's got his own mom and dad and his own brother.

I stop to catch my breath in the doorway. Ginny is there with a mask on. She pulls it off her mouth. "Good afternoon, Jerome," she says. "I was looking for you earlier."

"My cousin said." I stand there, waiting. "Did you find it?"

She pulls her eyebrows together. "Find what?"

"The piano."

"Oh, the piano. No. I doubt there's anything as big as that in the back room. Tom is still trying to find the keys."

"Did you check the basement?"

"No piano down there," Ginny says. "I was wondering if you'd like to help me sand the front room."

My back is tired and I have a blister on the palm of my hand. But it's my only way to get inside the mansion. And if I don't find Sharon's piano, I'm going to have to buy my own.

"Sure. I can help," I say.

She hands me the wooden block, sandpaper, and a mask. "Tom says we should start in the middle and work out."

Ginny pulls her mask back over her mouth and nose. I put mine on and crouch down next to her. I take short strokes with the sanding block because the grain is going in all different directions. The floor is made out of small pieces of wood in a pattern, dark, light, dark, light. This must be the mosaic Mr. Willie was telling me about. I clean off the wood with my sleeve so I can see what I'm doing. Small flowers, that's what it is, like dogwood blossoms all over the floor. Me and Mama planted a dogwood tree in the back corner of our yard, the white kind she liked so much because the blossoms look like they're floating.

Tom is in the hallway talking on the phone. "Yes, we need a dumpster. The biggest one you have. Make that two. One needs to go right next to the mansion. The other one goes next to the shack near the street."

I stop sanding for a minute. What shack is he talking about? He is discussing the price with the man. Finally they settle and Tom hangs up.

"When are they coming?" Ginny asks.

"Next week or the week after that."

Ginny is sanding away. "This floor is gorgeous," she tells Tom.

He whistles through his teeth. "Must've been a lot of work to cut all these small pieces."

Tom goes out to work on the front porch. But I need to know about the shack. "What shack did he mean?" I ask Ginny.

She can't understand me, so I take the mask off my mouth.

"Where is the shack?" I ask.

"Why, over there by your vegetable garden." She smiles behind the mask. "I'll make sure nobody tramples on your plants."

"Are you going to fix up the shack?" I ask. But Ginny can't hear me with all the banging. I shout, "Are you going to fix up the shack?"

"It's too far gone," Ginny says.

•

I sit by the door of the carriage house and wait for Mr. Willie. I have to tell him about the dumpster. I have to let him know. And I have to tell him about the lawyer, too. I'll ask him if he would be so kind as to adopt me.

Heat waves are rising off the blacktop, making everything all wavy. A mirage. That's what Mama called it when we looked down the road on a hot day and it looked like water but there wasn't any. A mirage can make you see anything, like now I see Mama in our garden with a scarf on her head and I say *It's too hot*, so she takes it off for all the world to see her baldness. A policeman stops and says *Is everything all right*, and I say *Yes, we're fine. Just fine.*

I lean back against Mr. Willie's wall. *Shack. Put the dumpster by the shack.* That way when they tear it down, they won't have far to carry the rubble. Two dumpsters, biggest ones they have. I close my eyes and then my fingers start moving, fast, up and down, a mazurka by Chopin, dance music, Mama said. Fast and crisp.

I wait for a long time, but Mr. Willie does not come home. The sun's so hot. I stand up and get the hose and water the four o'clocks and the vegetable garden. I spray water on my face and take a long cold drink.

The bag of cement is leaning against the front door. I dump some cement mix into the bucket, add a little water, and stir it around with the trowel. Then I start putting stones on the wall the way I've seen Mr. Willie do it, bigger ones near the bottom. You have to work fast before the cement sets. My part doesn't look as good as Mr. Willie's, but it's standing pretty solid. If we can get this wall done, they'll see the beauty in it. Nobody would tear down a wall like that.

# 23

After dinner I'm washing the dishes and Monte's drying when the doorbell rings. Aunt Geneva's talking real low, Uncle James too. "Yes, I understand. We'll be there. Yes, sir, in a few minutes." There's a police car parked in front of the house.

Monte drops the towel on the floor. "I told you," he whispers.

"Stay here with Monte," Aunt Geneva says to me, taking off her apron.

"Where are you going?" I ask, but they are already out the door.

Monte's doing his shaking thing again like he does when he's scared, so I get him a blanket even though it's summer and he wraps all up in it like a cocoon.

"Damon's in jail," he says.

"He's probably just at the police station."

"How-how-how do you know?"

I want Monte to stop his trembling. "Listen, Monte, we're starting your piano lessons," I say.

"Without a piano?"

"You'll see."

Mama said when she was small they didn't have enough money for a piano, so they made one out of paper and she practiced like that. But there was no sound. *Sure there was, Jerome. The music's in your heart and in your hands.*

I get four pieces of paper and tape them together. Then I take a black marker and a ruler and I draw a whole row of piano keys. I give Monte a marker too and show him which notes to color in to make the black keys between the white ones.

"Okay, this one here is middle C," I show him, humming the note. "So you put your thumb on there and start your scale. One, two three, thumb under, four, five, six, seven, eight."

Monte puts his hand on the paper just the way I show him and plays the notes. I sing the scale as he moves his fingers. Then I show him how to come back down, putting his third finger over on the E.

"Okay, now we're playing a duet," I tell him. We play the scales together, Monte singing high and me singing low. His voice is quiet but it's right on pitch. We go on playing all different scales and singing so loud we don't even hear the door open.

Damon's shirt is ripped under the arm. He's just standing there, not going upstairs or into the kitchen or anywhere, staring at our paper piano like that is about the dumbest thing he's ever seen.

"Go get cleaned up," Uncle James says.

Damon starts to say something, then turns and heads up the stairs.

"Jerome's giving me piano lessons," Monte says in a small voice.

Aunt Geneva's eyes are all swollen up. She kneels down on the floor. "Let me see, Baby."

Monte plays the scale.

"Very good." She turns to me. "I haven't forgotten about your piano, Jerome," she whispers. "I hope you know that."

I stare at the paper piano on the floor.

Aunt Geneva sits on the sofa and Uncle James is beside her. She is crying without making any noise, but we can see the tears running down her cheeks. "It's okay now," Uncle James says. "He got good and scared now."

Aunt Geneva nods.

"You heard what they said. He's young yet. First time in trouble. He'll come around."

Aunt Geneva covers her face with her hands. "I tried my best," she says. "I tried to raise these boys the right way."

Uncle James is rubbing her back. "You did a fine job," he says. "There's just lots of trouble out there, that's all."

"I tried," she repeats.

Then all we hear is sobs.

If Mama was here, she'd tell me what happened. *You can't make a plan without the information first*, Mama said. *You have to know the facts.* Suddenly I have to know.

"What'd he do?" I ask.

"Steal," Uncle James says.

"Steal what?"

"DVDs."

"What are they going to do to him?" Monte asks.

"There's a court date," Uncle James says.

Monte is crying. "Damon's going to jail," he says.

Aunt Geneva pulls Monte to her lap and then they're both crying. "Shhh," Uncle James says. "They won't send him to jail for a first offense." He looks at me. "Jerome, take Monte to bed. Best thing for him to do now is get some rest."

I look down at Monte. He's doing his shaking and shivering, but still we have to know the facts. "How did he get caught?" I ask.

"The cashier saw him put a DVD under his shirt. Caught it on film." Uncle James looks at Aunt Geneva. "We'll talk to Ms. Jackson. Her son's a lawyer and he can guide us through this process."

Monte reaches for my hand like a little boy and we head up the stairs.

# 24

Monte comes into my bed like he's been doing.

"What if they do put him in jail?" he whispers.

"They won't."

"He could die in jail," Monte says.

"He's right there on the bed," I say, "so stop worrying. He wasn't even in jail, just at the police station. And your dad's getting help from a lawyer."

"How do you know?"

"That's what he said."

Suddenly Monte sits up. "He's not all bad," he says, grabbing my arm. "You know that, Jerome?"

I nod.

Monte has his eyes squeezed shut. "I see colors with my eyes closed," he says. "What about you?"

I shut my eyes. "I see black and white," I whisper.

"I see purple and orange and blue. I see Damon's purple T-shirt and he's playing basketball and laughing."

I keep looking with my eyes closed. "No colors. Just black and white. Like piano keys."

"Are you going to stay here a long time?" Monte asks.

"You already asked me that."

"So you aren't going anywhere?"

"Like where?"

"Like New York. I heard Aunt Melinda saying she'd be happy to have you."

"I'm not going to New York," I say.

"But if you do, can I come?"

"I told you, I'm not."

Monte won't give up. "But if you go—"

"Your mom and dad are adopting me."

I said it. I let the words out of my mouth without thinking, like water out of a hose. Monte looks at me in the dark, afraid to move. Finally he grabs my arm. "I've wanted you to be my brother for forever."

I'm quiet then. Want has nothing to do with it. There's lots of things that happen that a person doesn't want. "I want to keep my name the way it is," I whisper.

"Because your name is something you're born with," Monte says.

"Yup."

"But if you don't change your name, can you still be adopted?"

"If you follow the process."

"What do you mean, process?"

"There's all this paperwork."

Monte is squeezing my arm so hard it hurts. "And after the process, you'll be my real brother, right?"

"If you stop digging your fingernails into my arm."

Monte relaxes his grip and looks down. Then he gets up and unfolds the paper keyboard on the floor. "I'm practicing my scales," he says, moving his fingers across the keys.

"Don't flop your wrists," I tell him. "A pianist is not a floppy rag doll."

He tries again.

"Better," I say.

He finishes the scale and looks up. "If I want, can I change my last name to match yours?"

I shake my head.

"Why not?"

"You just can't."

"But we'll still be brothers. Just with different last names, right?"

I never really wanted a brother or a sister. I had David across the street to play with and then I had Mama waiting for me at home.

"How come you're not answering, Jerome?"

I look down at Monte with his fingers still on the paper keyboard. "What did you ask?"

"Can we still be brothers even if our last names are different."

"Sure," I say. "No problem."

# 25

We go back to that lawyer and wait for over two hours. What'd he give us an appointment for if he's so busy? Aunt Geneva keeps shuffling the papers and looking at her watch. Finally I say, "Can I see those papers?"

"They're for the lawyer," she says.

"I know. But can I see them?"

She hesitates.

"Mama showed me everything," I say.

Aunt Geneva hands me the stack.

There's my birth certificate on top, Jerome William Mason. Place of birth: Cincinnati, Ohio. University Hospital. Next is my parents' marriage license. Underneath the date are their names: William Randall Mason and Sylvia Nicole Jackson. I wonder if Mama wanted to change her last name.

"When ladies get married, do they have to change their names?" I ask.

"It's the custom," Aunt Geneva says.

"But do they have to?"

"It's not a must."

"I'm not ever changing my name," I tell her.

She pulls her eyebrows together. "It would be simpler

if we all had the same last name, Jerome."

I feel the tightness in my chest. "Jerome William Mason is the name Mama gave me," I say. Jerome was Mama's idea. Daddy wanted to name me William Randall Mason the Second, but Mama said *Our baby isn't second, he's first.* When they came with the papers at the hospital, Mama wrote Jerome in the line for my first name. Sometimes people try to call me Jerry, but I don't answer because Jerry is not a name I like.

Finally the secretary calls us into the lawyer's office. He takes the papers and looks through them. On top of the stack is the one that says Mama died. I don't know why he even needs that, because why would I be getting adopted if my mother was alive?

"It looks like everything is in order," the lawyer says. He smiles at me. "It should come through in about a month." He doesn't say anything like *Sorry to hear about your mother.*

"Thank you," Aunt Geneva says. "It would be best to have it settled before the start of the school year."

"No guarantee," the man says. "We have to contact his father, you know."

I stiffen. My dad hasn't been around in so long. What business does this man have trying to find him now?

"His father hasn't been seen in years," Aunt Geneva says.

"I understand that. But the law says we have to make

an effort to contact him. He has one month to respond."

"And then?" Aunt Geneva asks.

"He can voluntarily relinquish his right to the boy."

The lawyer acts like he's not talking about me when I'm sitting in this chair right in front of his face.

"His father hasn't been present for most of his life," Aunt Geneva says crisply.

*A temporary stop. He's not interested in us, Jerome. No matter. We have each other, that's what's important.*

"The law protects his rights as a father."

"I don't know why he would have any rights after all this time," Aunt Geneva says.

The man smiles at her like she is a child. "Most likely he won't respond. That's what happens nine times out of ten."

Aunt Geneva stands up and looks him right in his face. "I hope you will do what you can to expedite this process," she says.

"We'll contact you as soon as we know something."

"We'll be waiting." Aunt Geneva leads me out of the office.

We walk down the marble stairs out into the bright sunshine. People are hurrying this way and that on the sidewalk. I can hardly catch my breath.

"Are you okay, Jerome?" Aunt Geneva asks.

Concentrate on each breath. In, out, in, out.

"You want to rest here a minute?" Aunt Geneva leads me to a bench in front of the courthouse. There's a patch of grass behind it with a sprinkler going. I let the cold water droplets land on my arm. Aunt Geneva wets her hand and puts it on my forehead.

"I know this isn't easy, Jerome," she says. "I know that."

The water is cool on my head, dripping down my neck into my shirt. *Water the garden deep,* Mama said, *to keep the roots from coming up. Early morning's best, before the sun rises. Then we'll practice our duet before you go to school, once the whole way through.*

Aunt Geneva is rubbing my back. "I know it's hard, I know. I know you miss your mama, Jerome. I do too, more than you even know, Jerome. There's a hole there for me too, but having you fills it a little bit." Aunt Geneva stops moving her hand. "I've been looking in the paper for a piano, did I tell you that?"

I look up.

"Uncle James says by the end of next month we may have enough saved for a used one, that is."

I take a deep breath, and we head over to the library.

"You know, when we were little, your mother and I used to come down here. Of course Sy was always reading those big books with big words in them. Your mother was smart, you know that? I always wished I was smart like that, but words never came easy to me."

I breathe in the smell of books and air conditioning and Mama. We used to say how someday we'd get one of those nice downtown condominiums that's only a quick walk to the library. Of course a river view would be nice too, Mama said, but we both agreed that the library was more important.

I check out a book about a blind boy and his seeing-eye dog, and another one about famous African Americans that I think Monte will like too. Aunt Geneva takes out one about how to raise boys.

"You already know that," I tell her.

"There's always more to learn."

"Now you sound like Mama," I say.

# 26

I wake up early and head up the hill. Mr. Willie's still not back. I water all the plants in the vegetable garden plus the four o'clocks, then I pinch the suckers off the little tomato plants the way Mama taught me. I wonder why they grow there if they aren't good for anything. I check the cucumber vine. Under a big green leaf is a tiny prickly light green cucumber.

Monte is there, following me like he always does. "How long until we can eat it?" he asks.

"Depends on if it rains or not."

"But you watered."

"Watering's not the same as rain," I say.

"Why not?"

We hear a loud noise. Two trucks carrying dumpsters are coming slowly up the street. One pulls up by the mansion and the other stops in front of the carriage house.

"They're tearing it down," I whisper to Monte. "For real."

"What about Mr. Willie?"

"He's not home now."

"I know. But we better tell them somebody's living in

there. We better tell them not to mess with Mr. Willie's stuff."

"We can't," I say, feeling my throat swell.

"Why not?"

"This whole place belongs to Ginny and Tom," I say slowly. "So they can do whatever they want with it."

Ginny is walking toward us. "Is this your brother?"

"My cousin," I say.

Monte looks at me like *Why didn't you just say yes*, but I'm not his brother yet.

Ginny reaches out to shake Monte's hand. "What's your name?"

"Delmonte," he says.

"Pleased to meet you, Delmonte."

"He's called Monte," I say.

"Monte, then."

Tom comes out of the mansion carrying three boxes that he tosses into the dumpster. The men follow behind with plasterboard and broken screens. It's hard to believe how much junk has been sitting in there, all smelly and rusty and broken. "Maybe they'll leave Mr. Willie's house alone," Monte says.

"I told you, it's not Mr. Willie's."

Ginny comes out carrying a heavy box. I help her lift it into the dumpster. "Thank you, Jerome," she says. "You're a lot stronger than I am."

"What's in these boxes?" I ask.

"Very moldy books," she says. "A lot of them. By the way, we went down last night and looked for the piano you've been talking about, but there's nothing like that down there." She puts her hand on my shoulder. "It's not as if a piano can really hide itself."

"Did you find the keys to the back rooms?" I ask.

"Not yet. But we looked in the windows, and there are just stacks and stacks of boxes."

I see Damon coming up the hill toward us. He stops a couple of yards from where we're standing.

"Another cousin?" Ginny asks.

"That's Damon," I say. "Monte's brother."

After I'm adopted, he'll be my brother too. I never thought of that before. I'll have a brother who talks back to his mother and shoplifts and smokes. But the adoption might not even go through. The lawyer wasn't sure. It could be that at the last minute my father will decide to claim me. He may decide that he doesn't want to relinquish his rights. But then what? There'd be plenty of places to hide in that big mansion. Behind all those boxes they'd never find me. *Breathe deep and steady, Jerome, count slow like the first movement of the Moonlight, slow and smooth.*

"Pleased to meet you," Ginny says, holding out her hand.

Damon hesitates, then comes just close enough to shake it.

"Looks like we got a whole crew today," Ginny says. "Anybody here who wants to work?"

"Yes, ma'am," Damon says.

Ginny looks him up and down. "How old are you?"

"Fifteen."

"You can help Tom," she says to him. "There's some heavy stuff down there to haul up."

I want to tell Ginny that you can't really trust him. He was just caught stealing and soon he has to go to court. But Damon is smiling and talking to Tom, acting all charming the way he does when he wants something. He says he'll be in tenth grade next year.

"What's your favorite subject?" Tom asks.

"Math," he says.

I never even knew Damon had a favorite subject. Tom wipes his forehead with the back of his sleeve. "I'm not too good at math, but Ginny here, she's good with figures. Isn't that right, Gin?"

"I'm not too bad," she says. She's squinting in the bright sun. "It'll be another hot day today," she says. "We better get started."

Tom and Damon go in through the side door. Ginny hands me and Monte sandpaper, sanding blocks, and masks, and we go into the mansion.

The small pieces of wood fit together just right, dark and light and dark, small flowers all around the whole room. I show Monte how to sand with rough sandpaper first, then medium, then fine to make the wood feel soft as silk. When we are done, Ginny gets some rags and we clean off all the dust.

"Take a break," Ginny says, standing back. "Isn't this gorgeous?" She calls Tom. "Come up here and just look at this floor."

Tom whistles. "Magnificent. Better get some serious varnish on it," he says, "to protect it for the next hundred years." He puts his arm around Ginny. "This is going to be the most beautiful school you've ever seen."

*It's not a school*, I want to tell her. *It's somebody's home. Me and Mr. Willie could fix it up and live here just fine.*

"Jerome and his brother did most of the work," she says.

I almost say *No, he's my cousin, remember, not my brother*, but Monte is smiling from ear to ear.

Tom takes out his wallet and hands me and Monte each twenty dollars. Monte is so surprised he can hardly talk.

# 27

The dumpster is already more than half full. Monte holds on to the edge and jumps so he can look inside. "Hey, there's a candlestick," he says. "I'm going to get it for Mom." He pulls himself up and over the edge. "Hey, Jerome, come on in here. There's all kinds of stuff."

It's hard for me to get myself over the top. Monte tosses out a crate that I use as a step stool, and finally I am inside.

Cabinets, blankets, lamps, pipes, screens. Mr. Willie said the house was just a shell, but really it's full of stuff. I pick up a wooden box that's small and white with green leaves painted in the corners. Inside are a few plastic beads and one of those diary books. I open the cover, and in curly writing it says *Sharon XOXO Wilson.*

I shut the diary quickly. I shouldn't be reading some-body else's private business, I know that. Underneath the box are a whole lot of moldy-looking books. I pick one up. *Catechism for Children*, it says on the cover. I open it to the middle and a dried worm falls out. I drop the book.

Monte finds a pillowcase to put our stuff in. Then I start opening every box to see if maybe Bach and Brahms are somewhere. We have to hurry because when the dumpster is full they'll drive it to the dump. All that dust gets me coughing.

"You boys better get out of there," Tom says, throwing in a stack of screens. "You could get hurt." He looks at Damon. "You want to start on the shack tomorrow?"

"Yes, sir."

Tom smiles. "No need for the 'sir.' Oh, and you know that book I was telling you about? I'll bring it for you tomorrow."

"Thanks," Damon says.

Monte's eyes meet mine like *Was that really my brother thanking someone?*

Then I almost tell Tom that Mr. Willie stays there, it's his home, not a shack, and after it's gone, he won't have any place to stay. But Mr. Willie might not want everybody knowing his business. Anyway, he hasn't been around in a little while. My stomach flips. Maybe Mr. Willie found some other place to stay, someplace clean and nice and far away from here.

I climb out of the dumpster first. Monte hands me the pillowcase and scrambles over the top. We carry it home together.

# 28

Damon eats like he's been starving, chicken, potatoes, green beans, pie. He's real talkative at dinner, telling everyone how Ginny and Tom asked him to help them for the rest of the summer, hauling, painting, whatever needs to be done. "They're in a hurry to get the school ready," Damon says.

Aunt Geneva looks at Uncle James. "The boy got himself a job," she says.

After the dishes are done, Monte asks if we want to play capture the flag, but Damon says he's outgrown that stuff.

"So what do you want to do?" Monte asks him.

Damon is standing at the door. He's wearing a jacket even though it's almost ninety degrees. "I'll be back," he says.

We sit on the porch and watch Damon cross the street. He reaches into his jacket pocket, takes out a cigarette, and lights it.

Me and Monte head up to the carriage house and wait for Mr. Willie in the dark. The air is hot, but there's a breeze in the treetops and it smells like rain.

"What if Mr. Willie doesn't ever come back?" Monte asks.

"He'll be back," I say, trying to sound sure. "If he left, he would've taken his stuff."

"When you left your house, you didn't take all your stuff."

"I couldn't."

"Why not?"

"They had an estate sale."

"What's that mean?"

"They sell everything."

Monte's picking up rocks and sorting them into piles in the dark. "Even the piano?"

"Yup."

Monte throws a rock far into the woods. We hear it fall through the leaves. "My mom had no right to do that," Monte says. "Because it wasn't even hers in the first place."

"She needed the money."

"Still," Monte says. "It wasn't hers."

We are quiet then, feeling the wind pick up.

"Jerome?" It's Miss Ginny calling from the mansion. We can hear her voice but we can't see her face. "Is that you?"

"Yes, ma'am. Me and Monte."

"Just checking," she says. "I thought I heard something out in the woods. You boys better be getting home. There may be a storm coming."

"Are you sleeping here tonight?" I ask.

"Just working late," she says. "We'll be leaving in a few minutes. Now go on home before it starts raining."

Me and Monte sit up in our room on the beds. The window's wide open and the wind is blowing. Lightning fills the room with the thunder close behind.

"I'm scared," Monte says.

"Me and Mama used to watch the storms come," I say. Mama always said she didn't want to live someplace that didn't have storms. *They make me feel alive,* she said, *like I'm a part of the world.* But even when things aren't alive, they're still a part of the world, like fossils and arrowheads and bones and dried worms.

"It could be a tornado," Monte says.

"It's not that windy."

Then the rain starts.

Me and Monte look at the library books. I show him the picture of Rosa Parks and tell him the story about the bus and how Ms. Parks didn't give up her seat.

"I bet she was scared," he says.

We look at her face. "She doesn't look like she is," I say.

"But sometimes you can be scared and not look scared." He turns the page and looks hard at the picture of Ms. Parks getting fingerprinted. "That policeman was wrong," he says.

"The whole country was wrong," I say. I tell him all

about separate but equal and Martin Luther King and the bus boycott.

"How do you know everything, Jerome?"

"Not everything," I say. "But my mother told me all about history because if you don't know where you came from, you don't know who you are."

The thunder is loud, coming quick after the lightning. Monte is holding on to me for dear life.

"You want another piano lesson?" I ask.

Monte nods.

"Okay. How about we try a real song this time. It's called 'Little Pony.'" I put my fingers on the paper keys and sing the tune as I play. Soon me and Monte are playing away on our paper keyboard and singing at the top of our lungs.

 **29**

Aunt Geneva has a big envelope in her hands. "Mail came early," she says, coming up the stairs. "And we got something from the lawyer."

Maybe Daddy decided he wants me back after all. You never know. Aunt Geneva sits on the edge of my bed, slits the side of the envelope, unfolds the letter on top and reads it out loud.

*Mr. William Mason did not respond to this summons concerning his son, Jerome William Mason. He has therefore voluntarily relinquished his rights as father and the case is considered closed.*

The case is closed. The coffin was closed. No nails or anything, just the lid was down.

"What's that mean?" Monte asks.

Aunt Geneva has tears running down her cheeks. "I know Sy is happy," she says, putting her arm around me.

How does Aunt Geneva know if Mama is happy or unhappy? Mama is part of the dirt now, so she can't feel anything. Aunt Geneva's arm is heavy on my shoulders, pushing me down into the mattress with the polka-dotted sheets. *Concentrate on your breathing, Jerome. That's right, in and out.*

Monte takes the envelope and reads the letter himself, whispering the words. "It doesn't say anything about adopting anyone," he says.

"It's a process," Aunt Geneva says.

I scoot away from Aunt Geneva and look out the window. Everything is clean after the storm. There are branches all over the ground, and the Jacksons' tree split right in half. The wind must have been stronger than we thought.

"Jerome wants his name to stay the same," Monte says. "And he wants a piano because you sold his."

Aunt Geneva's voice is so soft I can hardly hear it. "I know about the name, Monte." She takes a deep breath. "When Sylvia passed, I called a moving company for an estimate to move that piano to our house." She stands behind me, looking out over my head. "Two hundred fifty dollars." Aunt Geneva steps toward the door. "That's more money than I earn in a month." She clears her throat like she wants to say something else, then takes the papers and goes down the stairs.

Monte is standing next to me, so I can see the goose bumps on his skinny arms. Then he starts shivering like it's the middle of winter.

"Let's see if Mr. Willie is back yet," I say, reaching for my T-shirt.

·

I knock on the door of the carriage house.

"He's still not home," Monte says.

I push the door open and look around. The shirt is gone. The blanket is not on the mattress. Beethoven is not on the shelf. "He's gone," I whisper, feeling the wind go right out of my lungs.

# 30

The shorter man takes the first swing at Mr. Willie's stone wall. Two more hits and the whole thing crumbles.

I close my eyes, but I can feel the dust between my teeth. One by one, Mr. Willie put the stones in place, smoothing the cement, fixing that wall like it used to be. We have to show them the beauty in these stones, he said, the way they fit one next to the other like a mosaic.

"Good thing Mr. Willie isn't in there," Monte says.

"Be quiet," I snap.

Damon is looking down, kicking at the dirt. I want to say *Are you happy now, the bum can't stay here anymore*, but he's shouting to Tom across the street. "Did you tell Mr. Willie?" he asks.

"What's that?" Tom asks, cupping his hand around his ear.

"Did you tell Mr. Willie?" Damon repeats, louder.

"Wilson?"

Damon nods.

"No, I haven't seen him lately."

"Did you tell him that you're taking down the shack?"

"Tell Wilson? No, I didn't."

•

It takes less than an hour to level the carriage house. Tom and Damon and the men fill the dumpster with the rubble. All that's left when they're done is a pile of stones and a couple of cinderblocks. Me and Monte and some neighborhood kids kick around in the dirt for a while, but there's nothing to find.

"Let's go home," I say finally because my head is starting to ache.

"Where do you think Mr. Willie went?" Ashley asks.

Wesley shrugs. "Probably found some other shack to stay in."

"He doesn't have any money," Monte says.

"How do you know?" I ask.

"Everyone pays him with sandwiches and stuff."

"Not everyone. I bet he has money in the bank," I say.

"If he had money, he would have got himself an apartment," Ashley says.

"Maybe he liked this place better." I kick at a stone. "Maybe he wanted to stay someplace familiar."

Saying that makes me choke up. I want to go back to my old house, but there's someone else living there now. I could knock on the door and say *Mind if I look around? This used to be my house.* But a house is just a shell without the people in it. And Mama is gone.

# 31

In the afternoon, Aunt Geneva takes me and Monte school shopping. We go to three different stores, trying to find the lowest price for pants and shirts. "We can't have you two going to school in rags," she says, holding up a red shirt with a collar. The smell in the store is making me feel bad. I keep sitting down every chance there is.

"What's the matter?" Aunt Geneva asks. "Not much of a shopper, are you." She smiles. "Sylvia wasn't either. 'Just pick me out something, Geneva,' she used to say."

Finally Aunt Geneva settles on navy blue polo shirt and khaki pants for each of us.

"Now we're like twins," Monte says.

"Except I'm twice your size, remember?"

"Twins aren't exactly alike," Monte says.

When we get home, I have a stomachache. I lie down on the living room floor, and the room is spinning. I close my eyes. When I wake up, my throat is on fire. Aunt Geneva puts her hand on my forehead. "You sure do have a fever," she says, leading me up to bed.

I lose track of days. It could be one night or two, I'm not sure. Aunt Geneva comes in and out, and Monte too. I hardly open my eyes. Mama was sick for so long, sick from the chemicals they put into her veins. *Play me that song, Jerome, you know the duet we practiced for so long, the fast one by Grieg.* Over and over, one part, the other, together when she was strong enough to sit next to me on the bench. David and his sisters heard our music and came to the door to listen.

Aunt Geneva brings me juice. It hurts my throat to swallow, but I'm thirsty so I have to. Monte is lying still on the bed next to me, trying not to move.

"Jerome," he whispers.

"Don't bother him," Aunt Geneva says.

"Jerome. I have to tell you something. Mr. Willie came by. He was looking for you."

My head aches like it never has before.

"Mr. Willie said he'd be back."

"When?" I whisper.

"He didn't say."

I take a small sip of juice. "Where's he staying now?" I whisper.

"He gave me this."

Monte hands me a small piece of paper. I unfold it and hold it up to the light coming in from the window.

*Hello, Jerome. Your cousin told me you were sick. Just want to let you know that I'm staying at 8600 Reading Road. Come visit when you have a chance.*

*Wilson*

Underneath his name, he drew a staff with a few musical notes on it.

I shut my eyes again. Reading Road is a very long street. Me and Mama used to take the bus down Reading Road to the City Garden Center for our plants. *Besides the hostas, we could get some bleeding heart. What do you think, Jerome? We could get a few lilies too, for the back.*

When I wake up, it's the middle of the night. My mouth is dry, so I take a tiny sip of water. It doesn't hurt, and I drink the whole cup. Mama had to drink eight cups of water a day. *That's too much, Jerome,* she said. *I can't drink that much.* I said *But the doctor says you have to, Mama. Please.*

Monte has his leg over on my mattress. Damon's mattress is empty. I scoot to the edge of the bed and go over to the window. Something big and white is in the yard. I rub my eyes. Could it be a refrigerator?

I pull on my shirt and shorts, tiptoe down the stairs, and open the front door. The air is warm and humid. I walk barefoot across the wet grass.

He said it was a big white upright. That's what Mr. Willie said. He and Sharon used to play duets on that big white piano with Bach and Beethoven and Brahms looking on.

But how did it get into the middle of our front yard? If someone brought it in a truck, I would have heard it. I would see tire marks in the grass.

I look up at the mansion. It wouldn't be too hard to

roll a piano down this hill, one person to push and one to guide. It has wheels on the bottom.

I stand in front of the keys, set my hands in place, and play a scale. The D doesn't work and the piano is completely out of tune, but that's okay. I take a deep breath and start playing.

## 32

Uncle James pulls into the driveway and gets out of the car. "What's going on?" he asks.

"I couldn't sleep, and then I saw this piano."

Uncle James shakes his head. "In all my years, and I'm not young, I never heard of a piano landing in some-body's yard." He looks around. "I wonder how it got here."

"I think somebody pushed it down the hill."

"Somebody like who?"

"I don't know," I say. "It could be Miss Ginny found it."

"Miss Ginny?"

"You know, the lady who bought the big house."

"But why would she push it to our yard?"

I swallow. "Maybe because she knows I was looking for one."

Uncle James rubs his chin. "We'll have to get some more information, Jerome. But now what we need is some sleep."

It takes forever until I fall asleep. My mind is spinning in circles, but I want to tell Mama that I'm not mulling. It's just that I can't get tunes to stop playing in my head.

When I wake up, the sun is high and Monte is jumping around the room, chattering away. "Jerome, you saw it, didn't you? You saw we got a piano, didn't you? Daddy says maybe we can keep it long as nobody else claims it, and nobody has."

"Did you ask Miss Ginny?"

"She's not there. And nobody else claimed it. Nobody's going to claim it either. I tried it out, Jerome, I played the scales and 'The Little Pony' and I'm making up a new song, I want to show you." Monte grabs my arm. "Get dressed, Jerome, hurry up."

Ashley and Wesley are in the yard, and Ms. Jackson is talking to Aunt Geneva. "I didn't hear a thing last night," Ms. Jackson says. "Not a thing."

"Me either," Aunt Geneva says. "And to think that somebody could move something this big and keep it quiet."

"It looks in pretty good condition, too," Ms. Jackson says, "all things considered."

"I don't know much about pianos," Aunt Geneva says. Then she sees me. "Morning, Jerome. You feeling better?"

"Yes, ma'am."

"Do you know anything about this?" she asks.

"There used to be a piano in the mansion."

"Is that right?"

"A big white upright."

Miss Ginny pulls up in front of our house and rolls down the window. "Morning, neighbors," she says. "I hope I didn't scare anyone." She winks at me. "We found the key to the back room."

"But—"

She waves her hand. "No buts. If you want it, it's yours."

"But for the school—"

"Tom has a baby grand coming, used to be his grandmother's. Well, I better get to work."

She drives slowly up the street.

Uncle James, Damon, and I push the piano to our front door. "Okay, on the count of three, lift," Uncle James says. We hoist it into the living room. Aunt Geneva has cleared a spot for it along the back wall.

"You think we can really keep it?" Monte asks.

Uncle James considers. "Seems to me it was a gift to Jerome," he says.

"And now he's going to teach me how to play on a real piano," Monte says, placing his fingers on the keys.

## 33

My legs still feel weak. Monte's practicing the scales and I'm lying on the couch. Aunt Geneva brings me some ice water. "You sure you're feeling better now, Baby?"

I sit up. Mama never called anybody Baby or Honey or Sweetheart, but coming from Aunt Geneva, it sounds all right. "Aunt Geneva?"

"What is it?"

"Do you know where 8600 Reading Road is?"

"Eighty-six hundred, that must be down past Dorchester, toward town. What business do you have there?"

"Can I go there on the bus?"

"First you tell me your business and then I'll tell you yes or no."

"Mr. Willie stays there now."

I show her the note. She reads it over a few times and then considers. "I know you're eleven, Jerome, but I don't like the idea of you riding the bus to someplace you've never been." She puts her cool hand on my forehead. "Monte and I will go with you this first time. And then we'll see."

"Can we go now?"

"Who lit a fire under you?"

I smile, remembering how Mama always said that.

"Give me about an hour," Aunt Geneva says.

Aunt Geneva has a whole bag of stuff for Mr. Willie, two shirts, a jar of peanut butter, a jar of jelly, a loaf of bread, and two containers of chili. "He likes your chili," I say.

"That's what I hear," Aunt Geneva says. She hands the bag to me. "You ready?"

We get off the bus at the 9000 block, cross the street, and head south.

"Eighty-six hundred, is that what he said?" Aunt Geneva asks.

I'm holding the note in my hand. "Yup," Monte answers. "That's what it says."

It's an ordinary-looking house with a big porch that's sagging in the middle. We walk up to the front door and knock. My stomach is churning around. Mr. Willie might not even be here.

Monte puts his ear to the door. "There's music in there, Jerome," he says. "Listen."

I stand still and listen, and sure enough, it's a piano all right, a piece that's fast and light, like a mazurka, I guess.

"He's in there," Monte says, jumping so hard I think the porch might fall.

"Mr. Willie is not the only one in the world who can play the piano," I say.

When the music ends, a young woman comes to the door. "May I help you?"

"We're here to visit Wilson," Aunt Geneva says.

"The piano player," Monte says.

The lady smiles. "He told me he might have a visitor or two or three." She leads us into the hallway and tells us to have a seat.

A man in a wheelchair watches us. Two old ladies are sitting at a table playing cards. This can't be it. This can't be where Mr. Willie is staying. He had his own place with a mattress and a table and a bust of Beethoven.

I feel his footsteps before I see his face. "Welcome," Mr. Willie says. He looks embarrassed, like he's not sure what to say to us inside this building. "Thank you all for coming."

"Monte gave me the note," I say, "with the address."

Aunt Geneva takes the bag from me. "We brought you a few things."

"I thank you," Mr. Willie says. "I almost forgot to introduce you. I'd like you to meet Sharon." Mr. Willie enunciates each word. I see Sharon reading his lips. Then she smiles and reaches out to shake our hands. "This is the boy I told you about, can play the piano." Mr. Willie pretends to play in the air.

Sharon nods. In the light from the window I can see that she has piano hands, just like Mr. Willie said.

After that we don't know what to say. There are no rocks in here to arrange, no hose, no cement.

"Jerome's getting adopted," Monte blurts out.

I wish he wouldn't say that. It's my news, not his.

"It's a long process," Monte says.

"I know that's right," Mr. Willie says. Then he leads us over to the piano. "You know that duet we were talking about?"

"You mean the Chopin for four hands?"

Mr. Willie starts humming the first few measures.

"I know that."

"Let's give it a try," Mr. Willie says, sitting down on the bench.

"I haven't been practicing," I say.

"But now you have a piano, so you can get started again."

"How did you know?" I ask.

Mr. Willie laughs. "I have my ways."

Our eyes meet. "Really, it's Miss Sharon's piano," I say.

"Sharon's the one who told me you should keep it."

"But she doesn't even know me."

"Of course she does. I told her all about you. Anyway, what would we need with another piano here when we already have one?"

I sit down next to Mr. Willie on the piano bench. Monte's standing beside me, with Miss Sharon and Aunt Geneva.

Some of the old people are coming around. We set our hands on the keys. Mr. Willie nods his head, and we start. My fingers miss a note. I stumble. *That's okay, Jerome. Just listen and come back in. Let your fingers find their way. The music is in your heart and in your hands.* Mama said that. And Mama knew.